COOL
careers
for
girls

in

Air
and
Space

Also by the same authors

Cool Careers for Girls with Animals

Cool Careers for Girls in Computers

Cool Careers for Girls in Construction

Cool Careers for Girls in Engineering

Cool Careers for Girls in Food

Cool Careers for Girls in Health

Cool Careers for Girls in Sports

Cool Careers for Girls in Performing Arts

IMPACT PUBLICATIONS

COOL careers

for girls

in Air and Space

CEEL PASTERNAK & LINDA THORNBURG

Library of Congress Cataloging-in-Publication Data

Pasternak, Ceel, 1932-
    Cool careers for girls in air and space / Ceel Pasternak & Linda Thornburg.
        p. cm.
    Includes bibliographical references and index.
    ISBN 1-57023-146-X—ISBN 1-57023-147-8
        1. Aeronautics—Vocational guidance—Juvenile literature. 2.Astronautics—Vocational guidance—Juvenile literature. 3. Women in aeronautics—Juvenile literature. 4. Women in astronautics—Juvenile literature. 5. Vocational guidance for women—Juvenile literature. [1. Women in aeronautics. 2. Women in astronautics. 3. Aeronautics—Vocational guidance. 4. Astronautics—Vocational guidance. 5. Vocational guidance.] I. Thornburg, Linda, 1949- II. Title.

TL547.P276 2001
629.13'023—dc21

00-058119

Publisher: For information on Impact Publications, including current and forthcoming publications, authors, press kits, bookstore, and submission requirements, visit Impact's Web site: www.impactpublications.com

Publicity/Rights: For information on publicity, author interviews, and subsidiary rights, contact the Public Relations and Marketing Department: Tel. 703/361-7300 or Fax 703/335-9486.

Sales/Distribution: All paperback bookstore sales are handled through Impact's trade distributor: National Book Network, 15200 NBN Way, Blue Ridge Summit, PA 17214, Tel. 1-800-462-6420. All other sales and distribution inquiries should be directed to the publisher: Sales Department, IMPACT PUBLICATIONS, 9104-N Manassas Dr., Manassas Park, VA 20111-5211, Tel. 703/361-7300, Fax 703/335-9486, or E-mail: coolcareers@impactpublications.com

Book design by Guenet Abraham
Desktopped by C. M. Grafik

Contents

Special Introduction by Donna Shirley, Former Manager of NASA's Mars Exploration Program at the Jet Propulsion Laboratory and author of Managing Martians *and President of Managing Creativity.*

AIR CAREERS

COOL
careers
for
girls

in

Air
and
Space

Dedicated to all girls who dream of
flying and space exploration

Former Manager of NASA's Mars Exploration Program at the Jet Propulsion Laboratory, author of *Managing Martians*, and President of Managing Creativity.

Whenever I talk to groups of students about space exploration (which is often) and ask what they want to do when they grow up, they almost always want to be astronauts. Being an astronaut is indeed a very cool career, but for every astronaut selected, thousands of people who apply are turned down. But all is not lost! You should aim high. Even if you don't get to be an astronaut, while you are working toward your goal you will find many other jobs that you can do that involve space or airplanes. What are some of these jobs? Engineers, technicians, scientists, and pilots all work on spacecraft or space missions and with airplanes.

Engineers

Since I'm an engineer, I'll start there. Some people think that engineers drive trains. Other people get us mixed up with technicians and scientists. So what does an engineer really do? Well, we are the people who design and build the things that keep society working. We design bridges and buildings and figure out how to make sure they don't fall down. Aerospace engineers design airplanes and rockets and spacecraft and make sure they don't fall down, either. My degrees are in Aerospace Engineering. We are the people, for instance, who figure out what shape an airplane wing should be so that the plane can fly high and fast (for airliners and the space shuttle), or low and slow

(for crop dusters). Aerospace engineers also design the engines for airplanes and figure out how to build the structure that holds them together to be very strong but very, very light.

Aerospace engineers design spacecraft, too, which have to be even lighter than airplanes. Usually when you think of a "rocket scientist" (someone who designs the rockets that shoot spacecraft into space) you are really thinking of an aerospace engineer, who works on just about anything that flies. Other kinds of engineers help the aerospace engineers build airplanes and spacecraft. Mechanical engineers design the structure that holds the airplane or spacecraft together. Electrical engineers design the computers and the power systems that run all the lights and air conditioning on an airliner or that power a rover to crawl around on Mars. Chemical engineers help design the rocket engines and the jet fuel for airplane engines. Software engineers design the computer programs that tell the airplanes and spacecraft what to do.

Scientists

So what do the scientists do? Scientists find out about nature and then engineers use that knowledge to build things. For instance, chemists are the people who figure out how chemicals react with each other to produce lots of heat. Then engineers use those chemicals to make jet fuel and rocket fuel. Physicists like Isaac Newton figured out how gravity works, and now engineers use that knowledge to design trajectories that take spacecraft from earth to other planets. Marie Curie, who won Nobel Prizes in both chemistry and physics, found out about radioactivity, and engineers then figured out how to build electric power plants using nuclear power for spacecraft like Galileo (at Jupiter) and Cassini (on its way to Saturn), which travel too far from the sun to be powered by solar energy.

Scientists use the tools (usually instruments) designed by the engineers to find out more about nature. Scientists put instruments in high-altitude balloons, in high-flying airplanes, and on satellites orbiting the earth to find out about the earth's weather and what we human beings are doing to the climate. Scientists also use instruments carried by spacecraft to study other planets. For instance, Mars Global Surveyor has been orbiting Mars since late 1997 and has returned thousands of great pictures of volcanoes, canyons, craters, polar caps, and even dust devils on the red planet. Scientists are using those pictures to figure out why Mars, which used to have lots of water, dried up. Other instruments on Mars Global Surveyor are a laser altimeter to measure the depths of the valleys and the heights of the mountains, a "camera" which sees heat, and a magnetometer that can measure the planet's magnetic field.

Technicians

Technicians are the people who actually build the airplanes, spacecraft, and instruments, although engineers and even some scientists may get in on the fun. Technicians fasten things together. They bolt, solder, weld, and cut metal, and they wrap gold blankets around spacecraft to keep them warm. Technicians may run miles of wire inside an airplane or spacecraft to connect the computers with all the things that are switched on and off by the computers (like the instruments on a spacecraft). Technicians can also work with computers and software. If engineers or scientists have trouble with their computers, the person who will fix the problem is most likely a technician.

Pilots

Pilots, of course, are the people who fly the airplanes and, in the case of the space shuttle, the spacecraft. I used to be a pilot, and it's really exciting to fly. I flew little planes when I was a teenager—they usually went no faster than 80 miles an hour. Some pilots, like crop dusters, still fly small, slow planes. But a lot of pilots fly fast airplanes. The pilots who fly the shuttles are astronauts, and they fly the fastest as they whiz around the earth at thousands of kilometers per hour. Women have only recently become shuttle pilots. In fact, in 1999 Eileen Collins became the first woman to be in charge of flying the shuttle. But there are two kinds of astronauts—the pilots and the mission or payload specialists.

Specialists

The "specialists" are the engineers and scientists who operate the instruments and experiments during orbit. Some mission specialists are medical doctors who are interested in how humans and other animals can get along in zero gravity. (Zero gravity or "free fall" is what happens when a spacecraft is flying through space. An earth satellite, for instance, is basically falling around the earth, but it's flying so fast that it doesn't come back to the ground, instead it flies through the space around the earth. On earth you feel one "gravity." In space you don't feel any, even though gravity is really there, so you float around. If people or animals do this for very long, their muscles get weak and calcium comes out of their bones. So astronauts have to exercise a lot when they are in orbit.)

Other mission specialists "walk" in space to deploy or fix instruments like the Hubble Space Telescope. Others take pictures of the earth or launch satellites. The mission specialists do a whole variety of jobs, but the payload specialists are usually dedicated to a single instrument or experiment, because so much expertise is needed to operate it. Sally Ride was the first woman astronaut, and she was a mission specialist. Sally is also a scientist (a physicist) and has a doctoral degree. Most shuttle specialists have some sort of doctoral degree, either medical, engineering, or scientific. When the International Space Station is operational, most of the people who will stay on it (maybe up to three years!) will be "specialists," not pilots, because the station doesn't fly up and down—it just goes around and around.

So you can see that there are lots of cool careers in air and space. The stories in this book will get you acquainted with women who are practicing these careers. I hope their stories inspire some of you to be high-flying engineers, scientists, pilots, or technicians.

How To Use This Book
As you read each woman's story, you'll find a checklist with some clues about what type of person would be good in the particular area profiled. You'll get ideas of what a typical day is like and what makes the hard work worth-

while. There is information about what salary you might expect to earn as you start out and as you grow.

The final chapter, Getting Started on Your Own Career Path, gives you some advice from the women on what to do now. You'll find recommendations on books to read, some recommended Web sites, and a list of organizations to contact for information about student programs and scholarships.

Kathy Reeves

Kathy Reeves

Astrophysicist, Solar and Stellar X-Ray Group, Smithsonian Astrophysical Observatory, Cambridge, MA

Major in Physics, master's degree in Physics with Optics concentration, Northeastern University, Boston, MA

Astrophysicist

Sun Scholar

Kathy Reeves studies the sun, hoping to contribute to research that will answer the question: Why is the sun's corona so hot?

"It's a mystery that the corona is actually hotter than the photosphere, the layer of sun you can see with a visible light telescope," Kathy says. "The farther away you get from the sun's source of heat, the cooler it should be, but the corona, which is a layer farther out than the photosphere, is about a million degrees Kelvin and the photosphere is several thousand degrees Kelvin. What is the heating mechanism of the corona and why is it so much hotter than the next few layers down? That's one of the mysteries we are trying to solve."

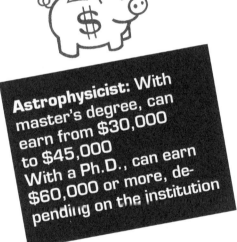

Astrophysicist: With master's degree, can earn from $30,000 to $45,000 With a Ph.D., can earn $60,000 or more, depending on the institution

KATHY'S CAREER PATH

Kathy works in Cambridge, Massachusetts, for the Smithsonian Astrophysical Observatory, which is connected with Harvard University as part of the Harvard Smithsonian Center for Astrophysics. She examines extreme ultraviolet rays from the sun, using a telescope to study images called TRACE-Transition Region and Coronal Explorer. The transition region and the corona are the sun's two outer layers. Kathy analyzes the image data from TRACE using computer programming to understand what's really happening on the sun. She also works on TRACE telescope operations. For example, she writes a time line for the telescope and tells it where to point and what wavelengths of light to look at. A third area of Kathy's work is developing the filters for a new telescope called XRT (X-Ray Telescope) that will be launched (in cooperation with the Japanese) in 2004 on a satellite called Solar B.

"There is a lot of visible light coming from the sun, obviously, but an X-ray telescope captures the X-ray light. To see the X-rays you have to block out most of the visible light with thin aluminum filters. I'm working on the filters and testing them to make sure they survive the launch of the satellite that carries the telescope."

What Kathy likes best about her job is the variety. She often gets to travel to Goddard Space Center in Greenbelt, Maryland, to do tests. She may get to go to Japan when the new Solar B telescope is launched into space. "In this job, I can do interesting science, operations, and design. There is always something different going on. Last week (the first week in

Biophysics internship
▼ working with DNA

Lab research
▼ assistant at Reed

Graduate school at
▼ Northeastern in
biophysics

April) I worked on the analysis of a flare on the sun that happened in late March. I was trying to analyze the data in time to submit an abstract of a presentation that dealt with flares before the deadline for the Solar Physics Division meeting of the American Astronomical Society.

"We analyze the temperatures in the corona and see how they relate to the temperature of the flare. We use a computer programming language called IDL, which is often used in earth sciences and astronomy. We can tell by the wavelengths in the images what sort of chemical composition

KATHY'S CAREER PATH

Switches from
▼ biophysics to optics

Studies the sun
▼ at Smithsonian

Observatory
▼

exists in the area we are studying. The flare wavelengths are mostly coming from iron emissions. Iron is being ionized several times and sort of glowing. (Ionized means an atom has fewer electrons than in its neutral state, which is 26 electrons. We're looking at iron nuclei with only 3 electrons, 23 times ionized iron.) The analysis I did shows that the flare is too hot to have the abundance of iron we thought it had. So we have to make some adjustments in the calculations of the abundance of iron with respect to hydrogen in a flare, to account for the hot temperature that we're seeing."

How to Predict "Space Weather"

"We are interested in these eruptive events because they are probably part of the heating mechanism for the corona. It's probable energy is coming from down below somewhere and erupting up into the corona in a flare. Another interesting thing about flares is that they are often connected with coronal mass ejections, where matter is actually blown off the sun and heads toward the earth. This is what causes geomagnetic storms and the Aurora Borealis (Northern Lights). Ionized particles in space hit the earth's magnetic field. These geomagnetic storms or "space weather" can knock out power grids and communications satellites, so we want to understand them as fully as possible and be able to predict when they might occur. We need to understand how flares are related to coronal mass ejections.

"Some of the pictures we get from the telescope are just amazing. The most fascinating thing about the sun is that it is a star, but you can really see what is going on up close. Most stars are too far away to do this type of observation. In the extreme ultraviolet light images you see arches and loops and jet-spray-type structures. The structures look very much like what you would see if you did a science experiment with a bar magnet and iron filings. It's actually the same phenomenon, because the sun spots are magnetic." (You can see some of these trace images on the Internet.)

CAREER CHECKLIST ✓

You'll like this job if you ...

Are extremely organized

Love math and will study physics

Are very patient and can wait a long time to get results from your research

Love to work with other people; science is about talking to others about ideas

Won't be afraid to ask a lot of questions to get the information you need

"My boss and two engineers and I flew to Goddard to run an acoustic test on the filters. These filters are very thin pieces of aluminum and they are very fragile. We want to make sure they can survive the launch. So we had a mock-up of the telescope and put our filters in it. We put it in a room at Goddard with two gigantic speakers. We played a simulation of the sound of the rocket we are going to launch the telescope on, and then we took the filters out and examined them for damage. We put a light behind the filter and a camera in front of it, inside a tube, and tried to see if there were any holes caused by the acoustic vibration." Out of six filters, there were holes in three, but they happened at the highest levels of testing. Two can be fixed by making the filters thicker; the other can be fixed by changing the material slightly.

From Biophysics to Optics

Kathy started graduate school thinking she would be a biophysicist. But during her graduate work at Northeastern University in Boston, she couldn't get excited about the research she was doing on the structure of hemoglobin molecules. She switched to studying optics and decided to take a master's degree rather than work toward a Ph.D. because she didn't have

"Astrophysics was something I had been thinking about for a long time. As graduation approached, I started looking at jobs in the field and realized I didn't have the computer skills I needed. I took some computer classes–C and C++

My parents are very supportive. They always told me I could be anything I wanted.

the compelling interest in the research she was doing to sustain her through the long Ph.D. process. An electrodynamics and astrophysics professor she had for a class agreed to let her do an independent study on astronomy and astrophysics. Kathy worked with the professor a little, doing computer programming of the data from the interstellar (between stars) medium. She was on a scholarship from the National Science Foundation, which she would have lost if she had left school or transferred to another area of study.

programming courses. These courses really helped me to be able to pick up the IDL computer programming language faster. They were indispensable in the work I do now."

The astrophysics professor knew someone who worked at the Smithsonian Astrophysical Observatory and mentioned that Kathy was looking for work in astrophysics. "I got the job through networking."

At some point, Kathy probably will have to decide if she wants to work toward a Ph.D. in astrophysics, because she can only go so far with a master's degree. But for now, she is having so much fun at her job that the thought of going back to school doesn't appeal to her.

Calculates the Edge of the Universe at Age 10

Kathy grew up just outside Denver, Colorado. Her father was an attorney who had a mining engineering degree and worked in mining law. Kathy can remember his explaining to her the theory of space-time when she was very young. When she was 10, her dad told her about quasars. "My dad told me they existed at the edge of the universe and helped me calculate just how far that would be, using the speed of light and how long it took the light to reach the earth."

Kathy and her dad would go out to lunch and her dad would draw physics problems on napkins. When she was in high school, Kathy took all the advanced placement classes—AP English (her mom was an English teacher), AP Calculus, AP Physics. But she never dreamed she would be a physics major in college.

After visiting a number of schools, she chose Reed College in Portland, Oregon. "The students at Reed

THE PROBLEM WITH LOOKING AT OTHER STARS IS THAT THEY ARE SO FAR AWAY YOU CAN ONLY LOOK AT THE WHOLE STAR AT ONCE, YOU CAN'T SEE JUST A PORTION OF IT, LIKE YOU CAN WITH THE SUN.

seemed so intelligent and creative." Kathy began as a psychology major, but she didn't really like it, and she switched to physics at the suggestion of her dad's cousin, who was a chemist. "I loved it. There weren't very many women in the classes, but that didn't bother me, because I had pretty much grown up around boys. I had a brother and our next-door neighbor, who we always hung around with, was a boy my age. It amazed me when I got to the Smithsonian that there were so many women astronomers. I wasn't used to seeing many women in my classes."

The summer after her junior year, Kathy had an internship which, she told her then current boyfriend, she couldn't believe they were paying her for because it was so interesting. She and some classmates worked with a pharmaceutical company to understand how a modification to the backbone of DNA would change its structure. The company was using the research for gene therapy products. "We came up with some interesting conclusions and ended up publishing a paper in a scientific journal. After my senior year, I spent a year working as a research assistant in that same lab and then applied to Northeastern for grad school."

Loves Cambridge

Kathy lives in an apartment right outside Cambridge in Somerville, and she can walk to work. She doesn't mind living with two men (one is a biologist and the other a teacher of high school math); it seems sort of natural to her. She knew one as an undergraduate at Reed and met the other through the first. On her days off, she likes to go rock climbing, sometimes in an inside gym where holds are bolted to the wall and sometimes in the New Hampshire or Massachusetts mountains.

Credit: NASA

Ellen Ochoa
Ellen Ochoa

Astronaut, National Aeronautics and Space Administration, Johnson Space Center, Houston, TX

Major in Physics, master's degree and doctorate in Electrical Engineering, Stanford University, Palo Alto, CA

Astronaut

Well-Suited for Discovery

In late May and early June of 1999, Ellen Ochoa flew in space to the International Space Station that is orbiting more than 200 miles above the earth. Ellen was part of an astronaut crew that reached the station in the space shuttle Discovery. Ellen's crew was the first to actually dock at the space station. The crew included seven people: a Russian cosmonaut, a Canadian astronaut who served as mission specialist, and five U.S. astronauts—a commander, a pilot, and three mission specialists.

Civilian Astronauts: GS-11 through GS-15 (depending on experience and years of service). Salary range is $45,000 to $115,000.

The shuttle flew above the space station so the station was between the shuttle and the earth, and then the shuttle docked on to the station. The crew transferred equipment and supplies so the first astronauts to live on the space station will have the needed

ELLEN'S CAREER PATH

Plays flute, likes math, graduates college

Gets master's and doctorate degrees in electrical engineering

Does research c optical systems, co-owner of thre patents

Credit: NASA

computers, clothing, medical supplies, cameras, and electronic spare parts. The Discovery crew also attached two cranes—a U.S.-built and a Russian-built crane—to the outside of the space station.

"I spent two years as an astronaut coordinating all the astronaut support to the development of the space station, so to actually go up and visit it was very rewarding and exciting," Ellen says.

As mission specialist, one of Ellen's specific responsibilities on the flight was operating a laptop computer program that plotted the trajectory of Discovery during the rendezvous

Learns to fly

Promoted to Branch
Chief at Ames
Research Center

Selected as
NASA astronaut,
marries Coe

using a number of navigation sensors. This program helped the pilots know exactly where they were in relation to the space station. Ellen also coordinated the transfer of equipment and supplies once the shuttle was docked, making sure things were transferred ment instead of having to use her hands to navigate her way along the space station.

"I really enjoy operating the robotic arm. I've been lucky to have operated it on all three of my flights. On the two earlier flights I was moving a satellite

THE CREW THAT WILL LIVE ON THE SPACE STATION HAS BEEN TRAINING FOR THREE YEARS.

in the right order so everything would fit on the space station where it was supposed to go. She then operated a robotic arm that held an astronaut who transferred equipment in a "space walk" from the shuttle to the space station. That way the astronaut could use both hands to carry equip- with the arm. On the flight to the space station I was moving Tammy Jernigan, the astronaut. She and I did a lot of sessions where we practiced together, so we had good communication. She knew what to expect from my movements, and I knew what to expect from the jobs she had to do out there

ELLEN'S CAREER PATH

Flies two missions
▼ in space, has a son

Flies third mission,
▼ works as CAPCOM at
mission control

while she was attached to the arm. It was a fun part of the training to get that coordination right. Of course she had to be really nice to me until she finished that part of the job," Ellen jokes.

Ellen says the International Space Station will play three major roles in future space exploration. First, labo-

Credit: NASA

ratories will be used for research in many areas, including medical practices and technology, new materials research, and environmental sensing. Second, the space station will be used to test technologies for human space exploration, including possible trips to the moon and to Mars. Third, the space station will promote cooperation with other countries to benefit everybody on earth. This cooperation should extend to other missions of space exploration.

Loves Math and the Flute

A native of California, Ellen attended San Diego State University and studied physics after graduating from high school. Although she didn't study physics earlier, Ellen loved her math classes and took as much math as possible in junior high and high school. She played the flute from the age of 10 and was in the marching band, concert band, and orchestra. "I still play the flute and got to take my flute on my first flight in space."

Ellen knew she would attend college, but when she got to San Diego State, she didn't know what her major was going to be. She thought she might major in music or business, but she took different classes to see what subjects she liked best. One was calculus. Other students in her calculus class were majoring in engineering and physics, and she decided to check out those fields. She signed up for a non-major physics class her second year of college. "I didn't have a background in it, but the fact that I had a good math background really helped me. I didn't have to worry about the math, only the physics part of it. Sometimes if you are trying to take physics and calculus together, you get bogged down in the math portion. But I could concentrate more on the scientific concepts."

CAREER CHECKLIST ✓

You'll like this job if you ...

- Are a good leader
- Are fascinated with lasers and lenses
- Are interested in how things work
- Enjoy doing laboratory experiments
- Like computers
- Will participate in extracurricular activities

In her math class, Ellen was studying Fourier transforms, which are formulas used to transform signals or images from the space domain to the time or frequency domain. She was interested in how the formulas could be applied to the field of optics. The physics department had a new instructor who was building up the optics program, and Ellen gravitated toward optics study. She did her senior project on the use of holograms to do character recognition. "They ended up keeping the set-up I developed and using it in their optics lab classes for many years."

Ellen got accepted to graduate school at Stanford University in Palo Alto, California, after graduating with top honors from San Diego State. In her graduate studies she worked on optical computing research and studied as a classical flutist, winning the Student Soloist Award of the Stanford Symphony Orchestra.

At Stanford, Ellen earned a master's degree and Ph.D. Her doctoral dissertation was on using real-time holographic material called a photorefractive crystal to do non-linear types of filtering. She and her advisors obtained a patent for a method to recognize defects in objects. For example, on a production assembly line the process could inspect pieces of equipment.

Wanted to be an Astronaut

Ellen applied for NASA's astronaut program at the end of her Ph.D. work in 1985. She was interviewed two years later but not selected. "Thousands of people apply," she says. Her first job was as a research engineer at Sandia National Laboratories, which is operated for the U.S. Department of Energy by the Sandia Corporation, a Lockheed Martin company. She was part of a small research team working on optical object recognition. She and her co-workers obtained two patents. One was for a way to recognize objects in an image regardless of their rotation or size, and the other was for a method to remove random noise in images using an optical system. "I enjoyed using the math and working with optical systems. My work was primarily experimental, so I spent a lot of time in the laboratory and got to work with holograms and lasers and lenses. It was challenging and interesting."

Space Computing

From her small research team at Sandia, Ellen moved to lead a research team in optics, going to work for NASA at the Ames Research Center in northern California in the heart of Silicon Valley. "This was a good opportunity to move up in my field and also apply my knowledge more to space applications. I was in that job for about six months and then was promoted to a Branch Chief position. I was head of a branch of about 30 people. They were all focused on how we can use computing for space missions in novel ways that might save on weight or volume. The research groups were looking at ways of doing computing during space missions, primarily robotic or unmanned missions. We were concerned about the restrictions that space put on computing capabilities, but we were doing theoretical work; we didn't have a direct mission we were supporting."

In 1989, Ellen once again interviewed to be an astronaut and this time she was selected for the class of 1990. She was one of 23 chosen out of 2,000 applicants. "I think it was a combination of my educational background and the fact that I had moved up rapidly in my career. I had patents, my articles were published in lots of research publications, and I was in-

Credit: NASA

vited to speak at technical conferences. Going to work for NASA was important, too—not that it is a requirement, but I certainly had a much better idea of what NASA did and how I could contribute after having worked there for a couple of years. I also think NASA was interested in people with extracurricular activities like music or sports, because it shows perseverance and the ability to learn different skills. As an astronaut you are asked to do a lot of things you probably never have done before in your career. I also had a private pilot's license at that point, which was important because flying is a part of our job."

Ellen had flown with her older brother, who had his private pilot's license. She decided she wanted to get a license, too. "It was important for me to know I could fly a plane on my own if I needed to, and I was just interested to see how flying worked."

Her technical background is very useful as an astronaut. "The first thing you do when you become an astronaut is to learn how all the shuttle systems operate. A good technical background helps you quickly learn how the propulsion systems, life support systems, electrical systems, and communications systems operate. You are responsible for knowing that as well as for understanding how to diagnose failures."

Up, Up, and Away

Ellen's first two missions in space were atmospheric research flights in 1993 and 1994. Her time up to the missions was spent primarily in training. "We were part of an overall program called Mission to Planet Earth, where we were studying the environment of the earth, not only from space but from the ground and from sounding rockets and other methods. The data we collected on orbit were complementary to data being collected from the ground and satellites. One of the main advantages of using the shuttle for the instruments we had was that you could calibrate the instruments just prior to flight and then calibrate them when you came back from the flight. After a

10-day orbit, the data we collected were much more precise and accurate than what you would get from satellites that might be in orbit for months or years. In fact the data we collected were used to help recalibrate satellites that were in space for a long time collecting similar data.

"We had one instrument on board called a Fourier transform spectrometer that allows you to measure two or three dozen different constituents in the atmosphere simultaneously. It's such a complex instrument that it is not one that would normally be flown on a satellite. That instrument brought back some interesting data about the constituents related to the chlorofluorocarbons that humans put into the atmosphere."

"These flights were fantastic. It was something I had looked forward to for a number of years. Flying in space is definitely the highlight of this job, although there are other parts of the job that are also fun."

When astronauts such as Ellen are not training for a flight, they have positions at the Johnson Space Center in Houston, Texas, that support the shuttle and International Space Station program. Right now Ellen is working in mission control as a "CAPCOM," the person who communicates to crews in orbit. She also spends a good part of her time seeing that simulations for space travel go smoothly. Her other job is serving on the selection board that is getting ready to select another group of astronauts.

Ellen calls La Mesa, California, her hometown. She met her husband, Coe Fulmer Miles, when they both worked at Ames Research Center. They have one son.

Ellen has received many awards. Among them are the Hispanic Engineer Albert Baez Award for Outstanding Technical Contribution to Humanity and the Hispanic Heritage Leadership Award.

Joyce Rozewski

Joyce Rozewski

Manager, Johnson Space Center Resident Office, National Aeronautics and Space Administration, Kennedy Space Center, FL

Major in Clinical Chemistry

Aerospace Engineer

Her Goal is "Go" for Shuttle Launch

Joyce Rozewski is one of the people who give a "go for launch" when the NASA shuttles take off from Cape Kennedy, Florida. (The part that makes it into space is called the orbiter. There are four orbiters: Columbia, Discovery, Atlantis, and Endeavor.)

Joyce sits at a 'management' console in the Kennedy Space Center (KSC) firing room. She wears a headset that has 8 channels feeding into it so she can listen to and talk with the team of engineers she works with. Together they resolve any problems with the orbiter that are their responsibility. "Like a switch is mistakenly left in the wrong position, or something either turns on at the wrong time or doesn't turn on when it should. It

Manager, JSC Resident Office:GS 15 government scale $82,876 to $107,738

takes us a few minutes to figure out what happened, but it is easily fixed and we can go on. Other times, there is not enough time to figure out what's wrong and fix it in time, so we stop or 'scrub' the launch.

"I consult with people at KSC, with people at Johnson Space Center in Houston (JSC), and with the people who build various parts of the orbiter in Alabama and California. Then I pass on our 'go' or 'no-go' decisions to the head of the engineering support management team, the Director of Process Engineering."

The whole point of Joyce's work (and her team) is to support the launch of the shuttle. "It is so exciting when it all comes together. The launch is a national news event. There are crowds of people. In the firing room I'm with the whole team of

people making it happen. We know the risks involved, and we hold our breath until the solid rocket boosters fire and separate from the orbiter. Then we all clap. It's a rush."

The Space Coast

Joyce grew up in Cocoa, Florida, with the space program in her "back yard." "My dad didn't work for the space program, but a lot of my friends' dads did. Companies and jobs came and went, so I lost a lot of friends because their dads would move away to other jobs."

Because of that, Joyce decided she would not have a career with the space program. In school she had many interests—ballet, gymnastics, math, English literature, French, and science, particularly the study of the human body. She decided she would

Hired as engineer, works
▼ on shuttle tile problems

Travels to orbiter
▼ recovery sites,
marries Greg

Quits after
▼ Challenger tragedy
in 1986, sells
pharmacy products

IT'S SO EXCITING TO BE WITH THE TEAM,

REVIEW THE DATA, GET PAST THE BUILT-IN

HOLDS AT T MINUS 20 AND T MINUS 9,

AND SEE A SUCCESSFUL LAUNCH.

be a doctor. She entered the University of South Florida in Tampa a math major with an intent to be pre-med.

"I found math too theoretical, so I switched to chemistry, which I found challenging." As she went along, Joyce realized that for her, being a doctor would be the single, 24-hour focus of her life. She found she could not do that because she enjoyed spending her time on a variety of things. She chose clinical chemistry,

a new degree program the university was offering.

"This is a combination of biology and chemistry as applied to the human body, and I studied additional subjects like physiology, microbiology, and pharmacology.

A Blow to Her Plans

The final semester in college, her advisor called her in and explained to

JOYCE'S CAREER PATH

Takes job with NASA, has daughter Katie

Works in firing room on shuttle launches

her what she would have to do to become a licensed clinical chemist. "He said I would have to work as a medical technician for five years. This had never been mentioned before. I was disappointed and rather lost, because that's not what I wanted to do. About this time I also broke up

with my boyfriend. I went home to Cocoa, brokenhearted and knowing I had to decide what to do about my future work."

Joyce had supported herself through college by doing secretarial work. She decided to take a temporary job at the Kennedy Center while she 'got her act together.' The temp job continued beyond a few months, and Joyce ended up doing engineering work. She had never known what engineers did when she was in college, but she liked the emphasis on solving problems.

The engineers were so impressed with Joyce's abilities that she was offered a job as thermal protection engineer and started full time with an international NASA contractor company that designed and built the orbiter. It was 1980, before the first flight of the first shuttle, Columbia. When Columbia was shipped from California to Florida, several of the protective tiles on the outside surface of the shuttle fell off. This was a serious problem.

"The tile problem created a lot of work for a lot of people. We had to take the tiles off, make them stronger, and rebond them. My chemistry knowledge fit right in—understanding the properties of materials, knowing about processes, mixing things, and chemical reactions."

"It was an exciting time and I got sucked into it—the teamwork, the new shuttle that had never flown before. The tiles were a new and untested technology. Would they work okay? The first time we held our breaths during the several minutes of reentry where we have loss of signal with the orbiter, not knowing if the tiles were really going to hold up to that tremendous heat and protect the people inside, or if they would fail and cause the orbiter to crash and burn. We didn't know for sure, but it turned out they worked well."

CAREER CHECKLIST ✓

You'll like this job if you ...

- Will learn to communicate well

- Can work well on a team made up mostly of men

- Are outgoing or will learn to be

- Will pay attention to detail

- Believe in yourself, not easily swayed

- Will learn how to present your opinions without being offensive

The Lone Woman

Joyce was the only woman among the 23 engineers on the team and got along well with her colleagues. (In fact, she fell in love and married a colleague during this time.) However, her boss was over-protective, which made her feel uncomfortable. "I wanted to be treated like one of the guys, but he treated me like a daughter. For example, I was a member of the recovery team, and we traveled to check out the orbiter when it landed. I could travel to California, but not to other 'dangerous' sites like Morocco, Spain, or Banjul, The Gambia. He never let me rent a car, I had to ride with someone. The final 'straw' was about my salary. I always got an outstanding performance rating, which meant I'd get a good pay raise. This particular time I was supposed to get a 10 percent raise according to the pay guidelines, but I got 3.5 percent. When I asked why, I was told that they had to downgrade me because there was another guy who needed the money more than I did because he was married. I was so angry."

PEOPLE RESPECT YOU WHEN YOU SHOW YOUR KNOWLEDGE, ARE SELF-CONFIDENT, STICK WITH YOUR POSITION, AND ARE NOT EASILY SWAYED.

It became clear to Joyce that as a woman at this company she could go only so far. She had requested cross training—and that was refused. Then came the tragic accident, the explosion of the shuttle Challenger in 1986. "I could see that we would be sitting around for two years doing 'busy work' while NASA determined what had gone wrong and how to fix it. So I quit and got a job selling pharmaceuticals."

Rejected Then Sought After

Selling to doctors was hard work and rather lonely. Joyce spent a lot of time in her car traveling from one customer to another. The doctors often didn't want to see her. "I was selling old products and they wanted to know what was new. I got a lot of rejection." After a particularly bad day, Joyce ran into people she knew from NASA. "They said they needed someone with tile experience and did I want a job. I said, 'Absolutely!' They started the ball rolling. Then my former company heard that I was talking to NASA and they wanted me back. So I had this competition going on between them."

Joyce agreed to accept the contractor's offer, but when she went for her final interview, they were going to give her a lower pay grade than they had negotiated. "I felt they went back on their word. So I told NASA what they were offering, and NASA matched it. It meant almost $6,000 more in pay."

A Design Woman

Joyce's work now deals with the design of the orbiters. She is at KSC, but is a NASA employee of Johnson Space Center, which is responsible for the shuttle. The folks at KSC do everything regarding launch, but Joyce works with the folks that design and build the shuttles. NASA is legally and financially responsible for the orbiters

"We used to have to approve every document before KSC could do anything, then sign documents after checking that work had been done. Today that type of attention to detail is done by the prime NASA contractors United Space Alliance and Boeing. My office is a liaison office at KSC, flowing information among the support team members and communicating with the Kennedy Space Center folks to solve problems and support the next launch."

Joyce, now a widow, lives in Titusville with her 9-year old daughter, Katie. On a typical day, Joyce gets up early, lets the dog out, and gets dressed. "I wear dresses mostly be-

THE ABILITY TO COMMUNICATE AND NEGOTIATE IS IMPORTANT. I'M A SHY PERSON, BUT I'VE LEARNED TO PRESENT MY OPINIONS WITHOUT OFFENDING PEOPLE WHO DISAGREE.

cause JSC culture is more formal (men wear suits and ties) than KSC culture, and as a manager I want a professional look. I wear hose and low heels or flats." Joyce gets her daughter's lunch ready, feeds the cat and dog, has breakfast, then takes Katie to day care at their church to wait for school to start. Joyce arrives at work about 7:30.

The first order of business is to check on the Daily Status Report. Every day the office prepares a detailed report about what has happened during the last 24 hours. This information is shared with all the support people. During the day, Joyce will have several meetings—check in with her boss at JSC in Texas, meet with engineers working on different orbiter systems, meet with a review board to sign off on current work solutions. If any members of the team need more information, Joyce helps get that information. When she's not in meetings, she has administrative duties and some special projects.

"I do travel quite a bit to meet with head office people and contractors. I was in Salt Lake City, Utah, to witness

the firing of a solid rocket motor. I traveled to San Antonio for a management review meeting." Joyce is usually gone about three days. Then Katie is taken care of by Joyce's parents, who live near her in Titusville. "I couldn't do it without their support."

On a recent trip, however, Katie went with Joyce. "I received an exceptional achievement medal in recognition of my work. I got to take Katie with me to the ceremony in Houston."

Laurie Leshin

Laurie Leshin

Assistant Professor, Department of Geology and the Center for Meteorite Studies, Arizona State University, Tempe

Major in Chemistry, master's degree and Ph.D. in Geochemistry, California Institute of Technology, Pasadena

Cosmochemist
Planetary Scientist

Mars Rocks Her World

Laurie Leshin is one of the few experts in the world on rocks from Mars. She has been studying the Mars surface and meteorites from Mars for nearly 15 years. She studied them through her undergraduate and graduate studies, as a post-doctoral fellow, and then as a professor in the Geology Department and the Center for Meteorite Studies at Arizona State University in Tempe. "I am interested in the environment these rocks came from, how minerals form, and whether they indicate an environment that might support life."

The daughter of a cardiologist, Laurie remembers walking into her father's research laboratory as a young girl and seeing a golden retriever whose chest was open on the

Scientific Researchers at Universities:
School year (nine-month) salary—range from $40,000 to $55,000
Additional income from grants to laboratories and research projects—average $10,000 to $20,000

LAURIE'S CAREER PATH

▼ As high school
student attends
college classes
with her mother

▼ Intern at Lunar
and Planetary
Institute, meets
astronauts

▼ Classifies
volcanoes on
Jupiter, studies
Mars surface

table. She could see the heart beating. "It's only looking back that I realize the influence my father's lab science background had on me," she says. "When I started college I didn't have a major. I was not necessarily the most focused person, although I had always loved math and science. But between my sophomore and junior year of college I had an internship experience that completely changed my life and from then on I was completely driven."

Grows Up on College Campus

At the age of nine, Laurie moved to Tempe, Arizona, from Phoenix with her mom and two little brothers. Her parents had divorced. "My mom is an amazing woman. She went back to school at Arizona State University when my little brother was three to get a master's degree in counseling. She often took me to classes with her, so I sort of grew up on the campus. It wasn't a big leap for me to get a Ph.D.; education has always been very important in our family."

Laurie's mom thought her daughter would be a good engineer. The first semester in college Laurie took engineering and a calculus course and was considering a math major. "But I decided pretty quickly that wasn't going to work. It wasn't scientific enough and it didn't seem creative enough. I had a great chemistry professor, and I was interested in the connections to the natural world. These connections were more interesting to me than the problem-solving aspects of engineering.

Graduates college,
▼ chooses Caltech
for grad studies

Studies water
▼ trapped in meteorites
from Mars

Post doc
▼ fellowship
at UCLA

"After I made the switch to the chemistry department, I started thinking about what sort of summer job I could get. I had worked in the registrar's office as a secretary the previous summer, but I felt like I needed to start working in my field right away. I was looking at the job board in February of my sophomore year and realized I had already missed the application deadline for many of the jobs. But there was one that said 'Lunar and Planetary Institute summer internships.' It involved all these geologic areas like surface geology that I didn't know anything about, but it didn't say anything about being a geology major. I went to see a professor of astronomy my mother had known to see if she could tell me a little about what the work might be like. My mother was always encouraging me to find mentors."

As it happened, the astronomy professor had been an advisor to one of the scientists in charge of the Institute's internship program. She recommended Laurie for the internship. "I went to the Lunar and Planetary Institute for 10 weeks in the summer. I was the youngest of 14 interns, one of two students who was not a geology major, and the only one without any geology background. I spent the summer analyzing data on the thermal properties of the Mars surface using information from the Viking Orbiter mission. The little building we worked in was near the Johnson Space Center in Houston, and it was where the astronauts would come to debrief after they flew. The scientists would have programs for us where they would talk about what they did, and I got to meet them. It was just spectacular!" That

LAURIE'S CAREER PATH

Leads astrobiology
▼ research at ASU

Adviser to NASA
▼ Mars Exploration
Program

summer Laurie was a co-author, along with her advisor, of a paper published in a scientific journal that discussed the work they did.

Laurie signed up for Geology 101 at ASU the following fall and asked the professor who taught it, Ron Greeley, if she could work with him. The advisor from her internship program knew Professor Greeley and told her to ask him for a job. Greeley didn't want to hire her, but when she got 100 percent on the first test, he changed his mind. So Laurie started working in the space photography lab at the college doing geological mapping of the planets from image data taken from the Viking Orbiter and Voyager, which had flown past Jupiter in 1979. Professor Greeley's group worked both on Mars data and on data from one of Jupiter's moons, the most vol-

canically active body in the solar system. The group classified volcanoes based on how they looked.

Experiments on the Chemistry of Mars

Laurie decided to remain a chemistry major, but now she was working for a geology professor, so she asked another professor who had responsibilities for both chemistry and geology if she could do her senior research with him. He was skeptical at first. She didn't have the mineralogy or petrology classes that a geology undergraduate major would take, but in the end, he said, "Oh well, you'll learn as we go along."

"I wasn't intimidated by not having the academic background, because I really just wanted to be in the lab, but when it came time to present some of the things we were doing, I really wished I'd had some of it. I ended up taking all these remedial undergraduate geology courses in graduate school. Maybe that's proof you don't have to specialize too early."

Her senior year, Laurie worked in the lab doing experiments on what the chemistry of Mars might be like. The work was chemistry, it was laboratory-based, and it was Mars research, so Laurie was very happy.

"Besides the sheer joy of being in the lab, one of the good things about working there is that when it comes time to apply for graduate school, you have a lot of people who know you and your interests and can point you in a certain direction. I knew I was going to graduate school, and I knew I wanted to make the leap into planetary science with a geological focus. My mentor in the lab said there were six good places to apply, because the programs were good and there were interesting people to work with at these schools. I applied to all of them, got into all of them, and got scholarships to all but the one that doesn't

CAREER CHECKLIST ✓

You'll like this job if you ...

- Like scientific experiments and would enjoy working in a laboratory

- Are fascinated with the planets

- Are excellent in math and sciences

- Will stay in school a long time to get the degrees needed

- Aren't afraid of having to raise money for your work

- Would enjoy teaching

give scholarships. I think this was because I had the undergraduate research experience, I already had authorship on a published paper (which shows you are serious about doing research), and I had good grades and great references."

Laurie chose the California Institute of Technology in Pasadena after visiting all six schools. She had a hard time choosing between Stanford and Caltech, but felt the students who would be her colleagues at Caltech were more compatible than those at Stanford. "They seemed excited about what they were doing, and there was a lot of extraterrestrial work going on. At Stanford I would have been doing more traditional chemistry."

The Water in Mars Rocks

Laurie initially worked in laboratory-based chemistry, because she didn't think she had explored that enough to figure out exactly what direction her research should take. Her advisor told her to look into the structure of hydrated silicate glasses. "Pretty quickly the first year I realized it was fine and interesting, but it wasn't fiery kind of interesting. Then the opportunity came to move to more extraterrestrial chemistry. This little conference came along about water on Mars. It was in San Diego. I was in the Los Angeles area, and I knew it wouldn't cost very much to go, so I asked my advisor if I could go with him. We heard some presentation that got us thinking about a project, and my advisor said he was going to ask the woman who talked about it to come as a post-doctoral fellow to work on it. I said, 'Well, if she doesn't come, I would be interested.' In the end she didn't come.

"It was a little idea that turned into a big project. I studied the water trapped inside these meteorites that we think come from Mars. There are about 25,000 meteorites in the world's collection right now. (Scientists request rocks be sent to them for study from collections like the Smithsonian Institute.) Of those, 15 are ones we think are from Mars.

They don't look much like normal meteorites; they look a lot more like earth rocks. They are igneous so they came from a volcanic environment, and they are quite young compared to most meteorites. Most meteorites formed 4.5 billion years ago at the very beginning of the solar system

"So the implication is that these rocks come from a large body, not an asteroid—they are young and yet they were formed from melted rock. The specific link to Mars comes from the gases trapped in several of the samples. When they were ejected from Mars in an impact event, these rocks

A FUNDAMENTAL FASCINATION WITH WHAT I'M DOING IS MY ULTIMATE DRIVER. I WORK REALLY HARD AND A LOT OF HOURS. BUT I ALSO SEE FRIENDS, TRAVEL, AND ROLLERBLADE.

and have been sitting on these small bodies called asteroids ever since. Not much has happened to them because the small bodies lose their heat really fast and the thing that drives volcanism is heat. If you are a small body, you can't hold on to that heat very well; you need to be a planet to have volcanoes going off over billions of years.

took a gulp of Martian atmosphere and trapped it inside the rock. We measured the composition of the Martian atmosphere pretty well with our Viking landed mission, so we know some things about the chemistry. It has a few weird properties, and we see evidence of these properties trapped inside these meteorites. It's as if a fingerprint of the Martian atmosphere

has been in place inside these meteorites. I would be extremely surprised if when we finally bring rocks back from Mars it is not obvious that these meteorites come from there. I don't know where else they could come from. There is not another gas reservoir in the solar system that could have given them this signature."

"It turns out that because of the kind of rocks they are, they don't have a lot of water in them. It is a difficult problem analyzing them. Also there is so much water on the earth that it's easy to contaminate them; you have to worry about this problem a lot and do careful measurements. We analyzed the water in a bunch of these meteorites and learned a lot about the interaction of the water in the Martian atmosphere with the ground and the interaction of the water in the ground with the rocks, and about the Martian interior. It turned out to be a really good project."

"The pioneering part was that we went in and looked at some specific individual crystals and analyzed the water coming out of them. We used an ion microprobe, a machine that lets you study individual crystals within a rock and keep the context within the rock, whereas if you grind the rock up you lose the context. It's a way of attacking the problem more systematically.

"The main implication people have jumped on is that water and rocks on Mars interact; there is water in the crust of Mars and it is interacting with the rocks. This is a very common geological environment on earth, and we found chemical evidence for this kind of environment existing on Mars. The reason this is interesting is that a lot of people think that life on earth got started in a hydrothermal kind of environment. Here we have some direct evidence that these environments exist on Mars. If we want to think about the possibility of life on Mars, it makes us optimistic that Mars would be a good place to go exploring for life."

Post-Doc and Professor

From Caltech, Laurie moved to the University of California-Los Angeles to do post-doctoral research. They had a brand new ion microprobe, the first in the world of the new generation of this instrument, and she wanted to use that great machine. "The post-doctoral fellowship is the best part of your career. You don't normally teach. You are smart enough and know enough to do things efficiently, and you have a lot of research ideas and not all these other responsibilities." Later, Laurie taught at UCLA in addition to her research. When she got offered a job as a professor at Arizona State University, UCLA also offered her a permanent faculty position. "It was hard to make a choice. All the personal stuff about coming home was really strong. Besides the ASU department is growing and that's something that I like. I knew that if I came to Tempe, I would be starting my own lab and getting my own research money to run it."

Laurie divides her time at ASU between research, teaching, and service. She is responsible for finding research grants so she can run her laboratory. One of her grants is from NASA's astrobiology program. "Astrobiology is

GROUNDBREAKERS
The Star Gazers

German-born Caroline Herschel (1750-1848) was the first noted woman astronomer. She discovered eight comets, the first in 1786. America's first recognized woman astronomer was Maria Mitchell (1818-1889). In 1847 she discovered a new comet, which was named for her. After her death, relatives organized an association in her name in Nantucket, Massachusetts, and built the Maria Mitchell Observatory there in 1908, and in 1968 the Loines Observatory was added to the site.

At Harvard College Observatory, Annie Jump Cannon (1863-1941) discovered more than 300 stars, making an outstanding contribution to the classification of stars.

In 1912, Henrietta Leavitt, an American astronomer, spotted a type of star that revolutionized the way astronomers measure distances. Cepheid stars have a light pattern so different than other stars that they can be used as reference points throughout the universe. Edwin Hubble used Leavitt's discovery to begin mapping the universe galaxy by galaxy.

Vera Rubin (born 1929) worked at the Carnegie Institute. Her measurements of the objects at the edges of galaxies became the major support for the widespread belief that there are large amounts of dark matter in the universe. In 1965, she was the first woman permitted to observe at the Palomar Observatory. She received the Gold Medal of the Royal Astronomical Society (London), the first woman to do so since Herschel in 1828.

Sources: Women's History Project, Stephen Hawkings Universe: The Cosmos Explained, Contribution of 29th Century Women to Physics Web site.

kind of a weird field; we have no evidence of life out there. On the other hand, it's fascinating, and I can't think of a more significant question to answer. We are looking at the formation of pre-biotic molecules in primitive meteorites."

Laurie's research work is focused on meteorites from Mars and also meteorites from asteroids. "These have a lot to teach us about the early solar system, before there were planets. They give us windows into the earliest geological events in the solar system."

Her service work includes the Mars Exploration Program. She serves as an advisor on a high-level committee that advises NASA on the best way to proceed with Mars exploration. "Even though Mars exploration is a small part of NASA's budget, it has gotten high visibility lately."

Laurie also must teach a certain number of classes. She is working toward tenure. "Tenure (protection from summary dismissal) guarantees your career at the university. It is thought to be very important for you to be able to express your intellectual views without fears of being fired. The goal of the young professor is to get tenure. The administration examines your teaching and service, but mainly it's how many research papers you are able to publish. The difficulty is finding the time to write the papers. With so many responsibilities, it is often hard to find the chunks of time needed."

As the director of a laboratory, Laurie employs four people who work in her lab. "The hardest thing is letting go of all the research. I am in the lab less now, and I don't get to do all the fun stuff. But I love the fact that I do so many different things in this job."

For fun, Laurie travels. She got to go live in Antarctica for six weeks to collect meteorites a few years ago and has been to Germany, France, the Czech Republic, Australia, New Zealand, and Hawaii. She also loves to rollerblade.

THE GREAT THING ABOUT MY JOB IS THAT I GET TO DO WHAT I WANT. IT'S SORT OF LIKE OWNING YOUR OWN BUSINESS BUT WITH A LOT OF INFRASTRUCTURE AND SUPPORT AROUND YOU.

Credit: NASA

Kathryn P. Hire

Kathryn P. (Kay) Hire

Astronaut, National Aeronautics and Space Administration,
Johnson Space Center, Houston, TX
Naval Reserve Commander Seventh Fleet Detachment 111,
Naval Air Station, Fort Worth, TX

Major in Engineering and Management, master's degree in
Space Technology, Florida Institute of Technology, Melbourne

Higher Flier

"**B**e prepared to take advantage of unexpected opportunities," astronaut Kay Hire says. "You never know what careers will open up in the future, especially in the field of space exploration." Kay is a good example of someone whose career took more than a few unexpected turns.

During her first year of high school, Kay's teachers convinced her to take the junior engineering aptitude test because she was so good in math and science. Then colleges started sending her catalogues. "That's when I realized I could get catalogues from any college I wanted." As early as the ninth grade, this Mobile, Alabama, Murphy High School student was ordering college catalogues from all over the United States, looking for the best engineering programs.

Civilian Astronauts:
GS-11 through GS-15 (depending on experience and years of service) Salary range is $45,000 to $115,000.

Naval Reservist:
Reserve pay is dependent on the number of drills performed

KATHRYN'S CAREER PATH

▼ Takes college prep courses in high school

▼ Studies engineering at U.S. Naval Academy

▼ Flies Navy oceanographic research missions

Credit: NASA

From her catalogue research Kay was able to review all the prerequi-

sites for the various college programs She focused on college prep and advanced placement courses such as English composition, foreign language, math, and chemistry. She decided on Georgia Tech because of its excellent engineering program. It was out of state and expensive, so she set out to find scholarships. When she met with a Navy ROTC representative to talk about money for school, he asked her if she had applied to the U.S. Naval Academy in Annapolis, Maryland. "What's that?" Kay asked. She hadn't heard of the Naval Academy, but when she walked out of the ROTC office, she had a Naval Academy catalogue.

In addition to sending in her application to the Naval Academy, Kay had to obtain congressional sponsorship to be eligible for admittance.

Every U.S. representative and senator can nominate a certain number of applicants. Kay was selected in tough competition by her congressman because of her good grades and school activities—co-editor of the yearbook and tennis team member.

A Great Education at Annapolis

Beginning college in 1977, Kay was in the second class of women ever to attend school at the U.S. Naval Academy. Both the male and female students came from the top of their high school classes. "The entire Naval Academy experience is premised on team building. The education was fantastic. It was a good, tough curriculum; however, there was a lot of help from teachers, probably more than in other schools I knew about through my friends." Students also were good about helping each other out when tutoring was needed.

"You couldn't just go to class and then go back to your room and hang out. You had to go from class to your required sports activity. I was on the sailing team, and we competed with other schools up and down the East Coast. There also were times when colleges from all over the United States would come to Annapolis for sailing competitions."

Flying as a 'Backseater'

Armed with a solid engineering background upon graduation (technical preparation for leading others in the Navy), Kay was one of the first women

KATHRYN'S CAREER PATH

Selected as astronaut

Flies 16-day mission in space

to become a naval flight officer. "The Navy had had women pilots since 1973, but they had just opened the naval flight officer position, the 'backseaters,' to women the year before I graduated. I wasn't able to train as a pilot because I didn't have 20/20 vision, but I knew I wanted to fly. I went through flight school and then was assigned to a squadron conducting oceanographic research. Women at that time were not allowed to fly in aircraft that carried weapons or would be engaged in combat. Although not combat missioned, the squadron I was in flew worldwide. I flew to 25 countries in three years."

YOU'LL FIND THAT MOST OF US IN SPACE-RELATED CAREERS HAVE MULTIFACETED BACKGROUNDS, AND THAT IS ESPECIALLY TRUE FOR ASTRONAUTS.

Kay's squadron collected data from the oceans by dropping buoys into the water, which then radioed back information to the aircraft. The Navy used this information for antisubmarine warfare and for other strategic and tactical purposes, but it also was made available to commercial fleets for mapping ice edges and finding out where an ice pack ended. It was used in scientific oceanographic research as well.

The plane was a four-engine turboprop, P-3, that could fly 12-hour missions. "That's why we were able to fly to so many countries." There were usually about a dozen people on board including civilian scientists who studied the ocean. Kay's job was to coordinate between the flight crew and the scientists to make sure the required data was gathered without endangering the crew or the safety of the aircraft. She also performed navigation and communications duties.

"The oceanographic research missions actually translated very well to my space shuttle experience later on. In the space shuttle, the astronaut crew truly represents the engineers and scientists and everybody else who put the mission together. The reason we are flying in space is to conduct the scientific experiments for these scientists. We are their hands and eyes in space, operating their experiments. I was already familiar with dealing

CAREER CHECKLIST ✓

You'll like this job if you ...

Are extremely focused and disciplined

Can learn very quickly

Are fascinated with flying

Enjoy working hard to accomplish goals

Will work at many different jobs to prepare to meet your goals

Will get an advanced degree

Will stay in good physical shape

Are good on a team

with scientists and trying to get the best information for them by the time I became an astronaut."

Shore Duty and the Naval Reserves

After three years of flying oceanographic missions, Kay moved to shore duty in California, teaching new Naval Flight Officers about navigation and communications. Because women were still not allowed in combat missions and it was rumored the Navy would probably decommission some of the few squadrons women of-ficers could fly in, Kay felt her career was restricted. "It was like training for something, then not being allowed to do your job."

Kay left active service and joined the Naval Reserves. She got accepted into a master's degree program. "I always felt the combat restrictions would go away, and eventually they did. When that happened I was right there ready to take advantage of the new opportunities." Meanwhile, she enrolled in graduate school to study space technology at the Florida Institute of Technology (FIT). She also got a job at the Kennedy Space Center in

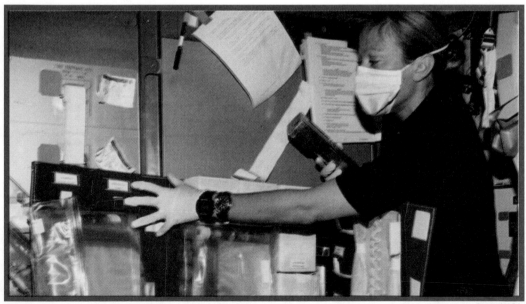

Florida as an engineer with a company on contract to NASA. "We worked the space shuttle from the time it landed, through all the maintenance and preparation up to the time it cleared the launch pad on its next flight. I had my hands in there on the flight hardware every day. It was a great experience." In graduate school Kay studied the different space sciences as well as launch operations, communications, and remote sensing for satellites. "I thought I might go on for a Ph.D. someday, but I don't envision I'll have time to do that now."

First Woman Assigned to a Combat Aircrew

When the Navy opened combat missioned assignments to women in 1993, Kay walked across the street from her duties at the Naval Air Reserve Tactical Support Center in Jacksonville, Florida (where she had been working with those who flew combat missions in the same type of aircraft she had flown in the Navy) to apply for aircrew duty herself. "It was an incredibly natural step because I already had a good 1,500 flight hours in the same aircraft, and all I had to do was learn the weapons system." She became the first woman in the United States assigned to a combat aircrew. As a patrol plane navigator and communicator she flew to Iceland, Puerto Rico, and Panama. Today Kay is a commander in the Naval Reserve.

"By being restricted to non-combat missions before, the women were also restricted in where they could go career-wise. But these days young women can go basically wherever they want and direct their career as they want. I believe the only places in the Navy that are still restricted are the Navy Seals and the submarines force. I expect someday that might change too."

In her studies at FIT, Kay prepared herself in case she was selected as an astronaut, a program she had wanted to get into for a long time. But she also enjoyed the work she was doing at the Kennedy Center and flying with the Naval Reserve. "It's never good to focus exclusively on being an astronaut, because the chances are pretty slim."

Aboard the Columbia

At the end of 1994 Kay was selected by NASA to be the first astronaut to come from the Kennedy Space Center workforce. She reported to the Johnson Space Center in Houston, Texas, the following March. "I've been an astronaut for five years and so far, I've flown one space mission, about two years ago. It was for 16 days; that is somewhat longer than the typical

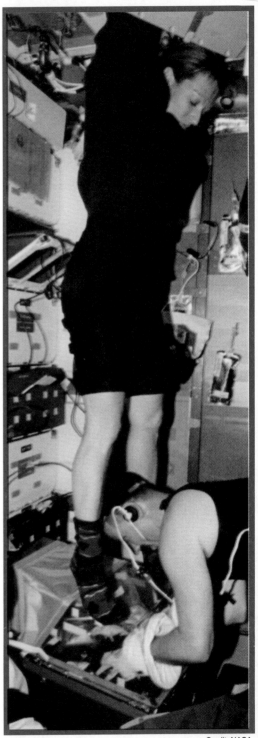

Credit: NASA

mission. Astronauts usually average about 10 to 12 years at the Johnson Space Center and may get to fly as many as six missions, but some move on to other endeavors sooner. A lot of people think we spend all our time riding around in space. While that would be wonderful, it's just not true. When we first get here we train gener-

May of 1998. As mission specialist 2, the flight engineer, she assisted the commander and pilot in operating and monitoring the space shuttle systems. She also helped operate 26 individual life science experiments that focused on the effects of microgravity on the brain and the nervous system in human and animal test subjects. Kay

WE HAVE FLOWN THIS SOFTWARE 97 TIMES, BUT WE CONTINUE TO MODIFY IT AND TWEAK IT TO MAKE IT A LITTLE BIT BETTER.

ically for any mission. Once we are assigned to a specific mission, we train for the tasks we will do on that mission. We like to have at least a year to train for a specific mission. Sometimes it ends up being a little shorter or a bit longer."

Kay's flight into space was on the space shuttle Columbia in April and

participated in lung function tests to check respiratory performance and visual-motor coordination tests in the microgravity environment of space.

Right now Kay is maintaining her airmanship skills by flying the NASA T-38, originally an Air Force pilot training jet. "I don't fly it from the front seat; as a mission specialist, I

GROUNDBREAKERS

The First Women Astronauts

The first woman in space was Soviet Russia's Valentina Tereshkova (born 1937) who spent three days in earth orbit in 1963. However, she wasn't a pilot and her ship was controlled automatically.

It wasn't until 1978 that NASA accepted women for astronaut training. According to *Working Woman* magazine, "Thanks to a few engineering advances, including a unisex, zero-gravity toilet and modular space suits that could be assembled to fit a great range of sizes, mission specialists could be men or women."

Six women were chosen from a field of more than 6,000 applicants that included 1,251 women. In 1983, Sally Ride, a physicist (27 years old), was the first American woman to fly in space. Kathy Sullivan, a geo-physicist (26 years old), became the first woman to walk in space in 1984. Judy Resnik, a specialist in electrical engineering (30 years old), died in the Challenger explosion in 1986.

In 1987, Mae Jemison became the first African American woman astronaut (at age 31). A general practitioner physician, she flew as mission specialist in 1992. In 1995, Air Force Lt. Col. Eileen Collins (chosen in 1991) flew the shuttle Discovery and became the first U.S. woman pilot of a space shuttle (at age 42). Sharron Lucid, a biochemist (age 35 when selected as one of the original six female astronauts), spent a record 188 days aboard the space station Mir during 1996.

Sources: Women's History Project, various Web sites

fly in the back seat, and I do not take the plane off or land it." She also spends time scuba diving and practicing space-walking underwater in her space suit. "We may run several different astronauts of different sizes through the tasks that will have to be performed on a space station assembly mission, trying to work out the best way to perform these tasks during the space walk."

Most of the NASA astronauts have technical jobs connected with the International Space Station as they train and await future mission assignments. Kay's current technical job is working on the space shuttle computer software. "I review the technical aspects of the software as a representative of the flight crews that eventually will fly it. We have flown this software 97 times, but we continue to modify it and tweak it to make it a little bit better. I work mostly with software engineers. We have a simulator we load the software into that looks like the space shuttle cockpit. I fly the software in there through all the different scenarios

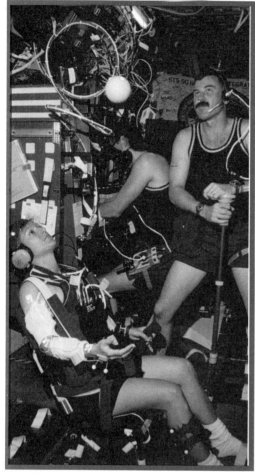

great team of astronauts, engineers, and technicians. We are making some exciting modifications to our software to try to make the space shuttle look more like the newer airplanes, going from gauges to computer displays. I spend a lot of time in meetings coordinating these modifications."

Kay has received many awards, including Space Coast Society of Women Engineers Distinguished New Woman Engineer, 1993.

When she isn't working, Kay is sailing or scuba diving. "I still sail; that started long before I went to the Naval Academy. I sailed as a girl in Mobile on the bay and out into the Gulf." She also likes to snow ski and to fish.

and make sure the computer displays show what I expect to occ.

"Let's say the computer sent a command to open or close a valve. I'm looking to see indications the valve moved in the correct direction and at the correct time. Before it flies, we have to verify the software for flight. It's a big responsibility, but we have a

Rachel Mastrapa

Rachel Mastrapa

Doctoral candidate, Planetary Sciences and Astrobiology, University of Arizona, Tucson

Major in Astronomy and Earth Sciences

Planetary and Astrobiology Research Scientist

The Ice Queen

When Rachel Mastrapa started her Ph.D. program in Planetary Sciences at the University of Arizona in Tucson, she wasn't sure what type of research she wanted to do. She had been fascinated with the stars since she was a girl. With an undergraduate double major in geology and astronomy and some experience studying images from Venus to try to learn about the planet's surface, she had enough experience to know that what she really liked was "the hands on" types of experiments that geologists do.

"What you really want to do if you are studying planets as a geologist is to pick up a rock and take it back to the laboratory and analyze it," Rachel says. "However, the only samples we have are the rocks that the Apollo mis-

Fellowship at University:
Doctoral student average
salary $20,000

RACHEL'S CAREER PATH

Takes advanced
▼ math and science,
elementary through
high school

Studies geology
▼ and astronomy

Analyzes spacin
▼ between cracks
on Venus' surfa

sions brought back from the moon and the meteorites that fall to earth. Many times, you have to work with images instead. A lot of people do photo geology—they look at images of planets brought back by satellites and try to

She got an internship at Brown University in Providence, Rhode Island, after her fourth year of college and worked with images from Venus sent back by the Magellan Space Probe. She tried to understand the surface of the

DON'T BE INTIMIDATED BY THE MATH. MATH IS JUST A TOOL. IT'S SOMETHING YOU PRACTICE AND THEN YOU GET BETTER AT IT.

figure out what is going on." Rachel had some experience with photo geology between her fourth and fifth year of undergraduate work. (It took her five years to get her bachelor's degree because she wanted a double major in astronomy and geology.)

planet by examining the patterns of spacing in large cracks on the surface. The evidence supported the theory that Venus is a planet with lava flows that periodically resurface the entire planet. "But I found this type of research somewhat disappointing. I

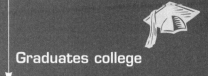

Graduates college

Gets fellowship to
Department of
Planetary Sciences

Studies Kuiper
Belt objects
through Hawaii
telescope

wanted to study the actual material, to get my hands into the experiments."

Rachel found a way to do more hands-on work and still stay in planetary sciences. When she started her doctoral studies at the University of Arizona in Tucson, she spent time with her advisor learning about Kuiper Belt objects (KEOs, also called EKOs for Edgeworth-Kuiper Belt objects and TNOs for Trans Neptunian objects; the names are controversial because there are disagreements about who first thought of it).

"These are chunks of ice that form a belt beyond the planet Neptune. They are at the very periphery of the solar system. The ice chunks range in size from small ones that are virtually undetectable to those that are kilometers across. The larger ones are observable by telescope. Water has been observed in these objects and that's why we think they are chunks of ice, but it's possible there are more components. The objects are so far away and so faint that you can't get a good enough observation to say what else is really there."

The Stuff of Life

"What's really interesting about the Kuiper Belt is that it could well be the material we started out with when the solar system was formed. Our solar system was formed out of a big cloud that condensed into a disk. Then the center formed the sun, and the rest of the dust and gas formed the planets. As soon as the sun turned on, it got really hot and heated the inner part of the disk. A lot of that material, when it formed into the planets, got

RACHEL'S CAREER PATH

Kuiper Belt
▼ composition
experiments

Does astrobiology
▼ research

processed, so it's not the original composition of the cloud we started with. But the area farther away, where the Kuiper Belt was formed, didn't get as much heat from the sun, and so it got to form at a much lower temperature. This could be the primal material of our solar system. It is conveniently frozen, sitting there waiting for us to look at it.

"My advisor was involved in observing what looks like a Kuiper Belt disk around another star. So it looks like it might be common to have these chunks of ice and dust out at the edges of any solar system.

"I'm doing experimental work mostly, rather than observing, although I have been to the Keck Observatory in Hawaii to observe KEOs with my advisor. But basically what I do is take gases that were available

at the beginning of the solar system and that I think might be there in the Kuiper Belt, and I mix them at various temperatures and pressures, and I see what kinds of compositions I can get. A lot of people have theories about what gases and pressures and temperatures would be in the Kuiper Belt, and I can test these theories. The studies that I've done have been with water, carbon monoxide, methane, and carbon dioxide. But there are also other gases that need to be tested."

Vacuum Chamber Experiments

Rachel uses a vacuum chamber at the Jet Propulsion Laboratory in Pasadena, California, to run her experiments. "We're building a laboratory like this in my department, but for now I have to use the JPL lab. The pressure inside the chamber is as close as you can get to a vacuum on earth."

Rachel inputs one of three gases plus water into the vacuum chamber where the temperature is between minus 253 and minus 70 degrees Centigrade. Then she uses a light beam to examine the results of the ice that forms. She breaks the light beam up into a light spectrum and measures the composition of the gases inside the ice. She also uses a mass spectrometer to count the molecules that come off the ice as it heats, so she has two ways to check her data—the light spectrum and the heated molecules. "The experiments I've been doing include varying the temperature and seeing how much water and how much of the other substances are there."

Rachel is observing "trapping" phenomena, where gases get trapped inside the ice in forms other than solids. That's because some gases freeze at temperatures lower than the temperature at which water freezes.

CAREER CHECKLIST ✓

You'll like this job if you ...

- Have curiosity about how the universe works

- Are able to put together and understand a number of different theories and facts

- Are dedicated to hard work

- Are independent enough to direct your own research

- Will have the patience to perform scientific experiments that take a long time

- Would like to stay in school a long time

- Will stick with your math and science courses

"When you are making a model of a Kuiper Belt object, you can actually get some of these gases at temperatures at which they wouldn't be solid. So there might be more volatiles in Kuiper Belt objects. What's interesting is that these components are very important in organic processes. Methane is the simplest form of an organic molecule (CH_4).

"A lot of people think volatiles (molecules that can change from a solid to a gas easily) are interesting because of their relationship to the origin of life. One process that can happen on a Kuiper Belt object or the surface of any icy body is that the methane can interact with ultraviolet radiation or radioactive particles that come in cosmic rays. When the gases interact with these energy sources, they can form more complex, long chains. Organic molecules are necessary for life. These could be the original components that were delivered to planets in the inner solar system if they got knocked out of the Kuiper Belt.

"There are people here who are doing research about the possibility of having complex organic molecules on a comet that smashes into the earth. Would it survive the impact or would it get too hot and melt? Some of the results are that some parts of the comet could survive. So you could get these complex organics onto the surface of a planet.

"Because we have an atmosphere here on earth, we don't get as much ultraviolet radiation and so it is harder to make these long, complicated chains. Some people think being knocked off a Kuiper Belt and traveling on a comet is one possible way for these chains to end up on earth. I'm not sure how I feel about that, but it's a theory. It's an idea scientists are kicking around."

Rachel's other experimental project is to see if bacteria can survive getting knocked off a planet and then hitting another planet. Rachel put bacteria in an ultracentrifuge chamber and spun them to about 436,000 times normal earth gravity, on the order of the amount of acceleration they might experience getting knocked off a planet.

"I like the experimental work. I can't exactly touch the samples, but I can set it all up and can watch the samples reacting. I like to change one variable and see what happens. I also like being able to collaborate with others to share ideas and research. I try to make predictions about what the Kuiper Belt might look like now if it started out in a particular composition, about how it might have changed. We scientists get together at conferences and argue about what might have happened. It's a very new field and there are lots of people interested in doing research in it."

National Science Fellow

Rachel has been on a fellowship from the National Science Foundation for minority students. Her father, an engineer, is originally from Cuba. She has applied for a NASA graduate student researcher's grant to continue her research. "It would give me a budget, and I would pay myself out of that for travel and living expenses. Scientists mostly pay themselves by writing grant proposals and getting grants, so

GROUNDBREAKERS

More Star Gazers

Who's Who of 1999 recognizes these two women astronomers: Carolyn Spellman Shoemaker (born 1929), currently working in Flagstaff, Arizona, has discovered 32 comets, including Shoemaker-Levy 9 which impacted Jupiter in July 1994.

Ann Louis Sprague (born 1946) is a space scientist working at the University of Arizona's Lunar and Planetary Lab, Tucson, Arizona. Some highlights of her discoveries and studies are the atmospheres of Mercury and the moon, and measurements of water vapor in Mars's atmosphere and in Jupiter's atmosphere following the impact of Comet Shoemaker-Levy 9.

Sandra Faber, professor of Astronomy and Astrophysics at the University of California, Santa Cruz, is mapping out major galactic movements that she is convinced are caused by dark matter. She and her colleagues, known as the 7 samurai, refined the techniques for analyzing the spectra from starlight. Her team can now get a three-dimensional picture of how stars and galaxies are moving in relation to each other. From this, they have drawn up a three-dimensional map of the universe and developed it into a computer model. One of their findings—our galaxy, the Milky Way, as well as some other galaxies, seem to be moving at great speed toward an unknown "great attractor."

Sources: Who's Who, *Stephen Hawkings Universe: The Cosmos Explained.*

it's important to find out how to write the grant in the best way you can. NASA has specific programs with specific goals. Right now Mars is really hot. Astrobiology is hot. My program fits into the NASA Origins Program, which is linked to astrobiology. I am the first person in this department to minor in astrobiology. However, if I don't get the grant, my advisor will pay me out of his funds. This department is really good that way. There is a general guarantee that you will be supported throughout your research, even though you might have to act as a teaching assistant to get paid."

During her first two years in her Ph.D. program, Rachel took courses, but now she has completed her course work and is involved in research exclusively. She also runs a computer laboratory for undergraduate students, which gives her some extra money. "I live in a house that has been rented by planetary sciences students for many years. The rent is $1,000 a month and there are five bedrooms, so when it is full we split the rent five ways, and it is cheap to live there."

I LIKE THE EXPERIMENTAL WORK. I CAN'T EXACTLY TOUCH THE SAMPLES, BUT I CAN SET IT ALL UP AND CAN WATCH THE SAMPLES REACTING.

When her research project is finished, Rachel wants to have a complete model that will show the composition of the Kuiper Belt at the beginning and what might happen to it over a long time. "The first part is mostly experimental and the second part is mostly theoretical. I use a computer to do the modeling."

After her dissertation is complete, she expects to get a post-doctoral fellowship at another university. "You find somebody in your field you would like to work with and apply to do strictly research. Post-doc positions last anywhere from one to three years to forever—some people like to hold that type of position permanently. You usually go through a couple of post-doc positions while you build your reputation as a scientist. You publish papers, present at conferences, and make sure others in the field know you are doing good work. Eventually I would like to get a faculty position because I like teaching. I like working with students, but I also really like research. The faculty positions are perfect for this sort of thing."

Rachel does find some time for her hobbies—camping, ballet and modern dance, and playing the violin. She also enjoys socializing with the 30 graduate students in the planetary sciences department. "Grad school is really hard work, but we have a great support system here. Just having people to talk to, to bounce ideas off of, and share experiences with is extremely important. If you are going to graduate school, be sure to look for a place where you will feel comfortable with the other students."

Mary Jayne Adriaans

Mary Jayne Adriaans

Member of Technical Staff, Jet Propulsion Laboratory, Pasadena, CA.

Major in Physics, master's degree and Ph.D. in Physics, Stanford University, Palo Alto, CA

Frigid Physics

Mary Jayne Adriaans has a *really* cool job. Her specialty is low temperature physics, with low meaning the unimaginable cold of outer space. It is called *cryogenic*—being or related to very low temperatures.

Right now she is working on a cryocooler project. Mary Jayne and a group of engineers are building a "cooler" that will provide a cool space for scientific instruments, sort of like a refrigerator. The cooler and instruments are scheduled to be sent into space aboard a rocket sometime in 2007. The cooler will be designed to work for two years at a constant temperature near 20 degrees Kelvin (or minus 253 degrees Celsius). "The instruments will measure the cosmic background radiation of the universe,

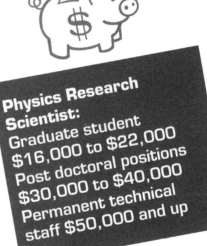

Physics Research Scientist:
Graduate student
$16,000 to $22,000
Post doctoral positions
$30,000 to $40,000
Permanent technical
staff $50,000 and up

'Nerd' who
▼ enjoys math
and science

Discovers
▼ physics as high
school senior

Works in physic
▼ lab in college

with a goal of getting a picture of its beginning to help scientists understand how the universe was created," says Mary Jayne.

Since she started her graduate studies at Stanford University in California, Mary Jayne has been working with low-temperature physics. She designed and built an instrument that could measure the properties of liquid helium at very cold temperatures. To do this, she built precise thermometers, used machines (lathe, mill, drill press), did leak-free plumbing (soldering and brazing), developed electronics, and created software for data analysis. "The thermometers that I constructed can measure temperature differences of one-billionth of a degree." (That is 0.000000001 degree.)

What Mary Jayne likes best in her work is building something from

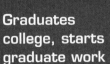
the ground up. "It is exciting to start with nothing and with your own hands build something that does what you want it to. I enjoy all the hands-on work—the wiring, soldering, machining, and making instruments work in a vacuum. The work is so rewarding."

A Southern California Gal

Mary Jayne grew up in southern California, enjoyed school, and says she was definitely a 'nerd' in high school. "One big advantage I had growing up—no one ever told me that math and science were something I couldn't do. In the 1970s that was an unusual experience. At first, I wanted to be a lawyer, but when I started high school I discovered lawyering involved public speaking. I was very shy and didn't think I could do that. I realized that I enjoyed (and was pretty good at) math and science. I took as many courses as I could, even went to the University of California at Irvine my senior year for a calculus class. Also that year I took my first physics class, loved it, and decided that would be my major when I started college."

While in college, Mary Jayne got a job in a physics lab for two years. "I did very basic lab work to help graduate students. I discovered what it was like to work in a lab." About that same time, she visited the career center to check out what kind of jobs a physics major could get upon graduation. "I discovered all the jobs I found interesting, like working in aerospace, required a doctoral degree. So I knew then I would be going to graduate school. I applied early in my senior year, got accepted to several graduate schools, and chose Stanford because it had the facilities I wanted, and it felt comfortable, most like home."

on ($16,000 at the beginning and $20,000 by the time she got her degree). Most technical graduate schools are that way; they pay a 'survival' wage while you study. You earn it by

I ENJOY BUILDING THE EXPERIMENT, THE PRECISE, DETAILED WORK, AND CREATING SOMETHING THAT DOES THIS INCREDIBLE MEASUREMENT.

Independent Study

Up to this time, Mary Jayne had lived at home, which allowed her to cut expenses. Her four-year scholarship of $2,000 per year covered most of her undergraduate tuition costs. "As a grad student, I earned enough to live

working for professors who usually get funding from outside the university for their research. This work becomes part of your doctoral thesis.

"The first two years are coursework and teaching. Then comes your independent research—creating and then publishing original work. The idea was a bit frightening when I started. I wasn't sure I could do it. But I gained confidence and found the coursework was the hardest and the research the most enjoyable."

Mary Jayne's independent work choice, decided upon with the help of her faculty advisor, was to develop an experiment that would measure a property of liquid helium more precisely than had ever been done before. "I was looking for a research project, and this sounded like the hands-on work I'd be interested in."

A NASA Experiment

The next step after getting a Ph.D. is to apply for a post-doctoral position. This is like a doctor's residency or a technical apprenticeship—the scientist gets experience and works toward a permanent staff position. Mary Jayne got offers for several post-doctoral positions and chose Sandia National Laboratories, Albuquerque, New Mexico.

"I continued doing work similar to my thesis, and I worked in a lab on the

CAREER CHECKLIST ✓

You'll like this job if you ...

Love physics

Like to work in a laboratory

Pay attention to details

Like hands-on work

Will stick to something, not quit

Will get the advanced degrees necessary

Will learn to write and speak well

campus of the University of New Mexico. We worked on a NASA-sponsored experiment that would fly aboard the space shuttle. The instruments have to handle low temperatures and not be affected by the vibrations during a shuttle launch." Mary Jayne helped make improvements in building low-temperature thermometers in order to make more precise measurements on earth and in space.

Mary Jayne became a permanent staff member at Sandia and had PI (principal investigator) duties on three projects. The funding of her projects changed, and then she got involved in defense work. "This was not the fundamental physics work and hands-on work that I liked and had been trained to do. Some of the associates I'd been working closely with were from the Jet Propulsion Lab. (JPL is run by the California Institute of Technology for NASA and had oversight on some of her previous work.) They began suggesting I come to work at JPL. They sent me lists of job openings. I applied and was finally hired in 1998."

Her Day at Jet Propulsion Laboratory

When Mary Jayne joined JPL, she began again to work in the area of low-temperature physics and with experiments to be conducted on the International Space Station. On a typical day, she gets up at early, starts most of her days with a run, showers, and gets to work around 9 a.m.

The first morning work tasks are checking and answering messages, then going to meetings with coworkers to discuss the work to be done.

THE THERMOMETERS THAT I DESIGNED AND CONSTRUCTED COULD MEASURE ONE-BILLIONTH OF A DEGREE.

"At the beginning of any project there is a lot of planning. After that comes the hands-on work. Soon I'll be spending days in the laboratory, building a test facility. We do the design on computers, and for building large hardware like the vacuum chamber, we will hire an outside contractor. But most of the assembly, basic plumbing, and wiring will be done at JPL."

Mary Jayne leaves between 5 and 6 p.m. and returns to her three-bedroom home. Once or twice a week she pilots an airplane. "When I was a kid, I went up with my dad when he learned to fly, and I loved it. When I was in New Mexico, I finally could afford lessons. I got my license in 1998 and now am working on my instrument rating."

Recently Mary Jayne trained for a marathon. "I've gotten hooked on running. I'm proud of finishing my first marathon. I did the 26.2 miles in 4 hours and 48 minutes and finished in the top 20 percent of women runners. It is the hardest physical thing I have ever done. We ran in the rain, and it was cold and wet. It reminded me a bit of my research. You have to stick to it, never even think of quitting."

Mary Jayne has applied to NASA to become an astronaut and made the first cut. For Mary Jayne, "giving up is not an option if you want to succeed" in this cool, cool job.

Credit: Carolyn Russo

Bonnie Wilkens

Bonnie Wilkens

Pilot, AgRotors, Gettysburg, PA.

Major in Zoology, master's degree in Bio-Aeronautics

Helicopter Pilot

Up, Down, and Sideways

"Flying a helicopter requires your complete attention. You can't sit back and put it on automatic pilot. You are constantly using your hands, feet, eyes, and ears. I love it," says Bonnie Wilkens. She uses her flying skills to spray water on forest fires and chemicals on agricultural crops and on such pest problems as the gypsy moth or spruce bugworm—caterpillers that devour entire forests, killing trees by eating their foliage. Other sprays kill herbaceous weeds and mosquitoes.

Bonnie didn't even know a job like hers existed until, as a requirement of her master's degree work, she was assigned to an agriculture spraying company as a student intern. The

Helicopter Pilot:
Salaries vary depending on the company, type of mission flown, and type of helicopter flown. Inexperienced pilots expect low wage and nonpilot duties.
Beginning pilots (piston): $19,000 to $55,000
Rotor & Wing magazine

Firefighter: $37,650 to $110,000
Note: U.S. Forest Service has a special firefighting service based in Boise, Idaho. The state of California handles firefighting in California forests. Private contractors supplement all these services.

BONNIE'S CAREER PATH

Wants to be
veterinarian,
studies zoology

Takes up parachuting,
studies bio-aeronautics

Learns to fly,
interns at
AgRotors

company used helicopters rather than the small, single engine airplanes that most crop-spraying companies used.

"It was so exciting to be able to stop, back up, do those things you can't do in a regular airplane. It was very unstable, and I even enjoyed that, as it was a challenge."

From Zoology to Bio-Aeronautics

When Bonnie was a girl in New Hampshire, she wanted to be a veterinarian. Her mother was English and returned to England with Bonnie and her two sisters when Bonnie's father died. In England, Bonnie took science courses and worked hard because she knew it was difficult to get into veterinary school. During the summers, she visited her aunt in New York and took waitressing jobs to earn money for school.

When Bonnie was 16, she and 11 other girls earned a place in the two-year, A-level program at a prestigious boys' school (Blundells in Devon, England, of Lorna Doone fame). She studied physics, chemistry, and biology. "This school also offered a great sports program, much greater choices that we girls had ever had. One choice was parachuting. I fell in love with the sport. I loved the airports, the taking off, the jumps, sky diving."

Bonnie finished her two years at Blundells, then went to Cardiff (South Wales) for three years to get a bachelor's degree in zoology. "During this time I skydived and realized I wanted to pursue a career in aviation." After graduating, Bonnie enrolled for a master's degree, studying bio-aeronautics—the study of agriculture and aerial spraying to control bugs, fungi, and nutrient deficiencies in plants. She learned to fly a single-engine plane,

"As students, we worked as part of the ground support crew. Each helicopter needs a crew on the ground to follow the aircraft from place to place. We helped with fueling, loading and

IN THIS MALE-DOMINATED FIELD, I'M 'ONE OF THE GUYS.' I DON'T EXPECT ANY SPECIAL TREATMENT, BUT MAKE SURE I'M PULLING MY SHARE OF THE LOAD.

and she learned about mixing and loading chemicals and how the spray operations worked. As part of the training to get a master's degree, bio-aeronautics students were assigned to companies in various locations around the world where spraying took place. Bonnie came to Pennsylvania and the AgRotors company.

mixing chemicals, driving the trucks, carrying boxes of supplies, helping the mechanic—whatever was needed."

Bonnie returned to school to finish her degree. She decided what she wanted to do was become a helicopter pilot and fly spray missions. She got her degree in October, then visited her aunt and worked waitressing jobs in New York City to raise money. Back in England for Christmas, she knew she would have to borrow money to get pilot training.

"My mom, who works as a special needs teacher, is really supportive. When I told her I felt this was the right thing for me, she sold the family home to get the money. Learning to fly can be expensive. Flight training and fuel costs are high, and it takes lots of flying hours to get a license. It was an enormous debt for me, $28,000, especially as I'd never been in debt before. I've paid it all back now, and I appreciate how my mother believed in me. To

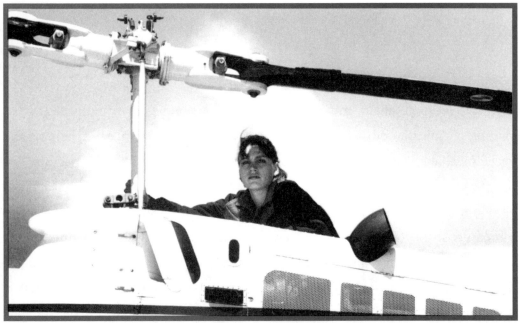

Credit: Carolyn Russo

tell the truth, it never occurred to me that I wouldn't succeed and be able to pay her back."

Flight Training Hard

After the holiday season, Bonnie returned to the Gettysburg area and her friends at AgRotors. "I decided to do my flight training there because I liked the people. There was no contract or promise of subsequent work, and I spent my time learning how to fly for four solid months.

"I have always liked a challenge, and learning to fly the helicopter certainly provided me with that. Hovering was hard to learn, as each control affects another, and it takes a while to figure out what causes which motion. I particularly enjoyed the slow speed flight, hovering maneuvers, backing up, and sideward flight—probably as I couldn't do that in an airplane. After this training, AgRotors offered me a job working in ground support. It was a great opportunity for me."

"Agricultural aerial spraying is such unique work that you learn best

CAREER CHECKLIST ✓

You'll like this job if you ...

Prefer being outdoors

Like a challenge

Are willing to work long hours

Can work as a team member, doing any type of job needed

Can get along with all kinds of people

Are safety minded

Can entertain yourself when there's 'nothing to do'

by helping out in all the operations—I learned maintenance work, drove the truck, ran errands to get parts."

While Bonnie was working ground support, the company gave her some

THE HELICOPTER IS UNSTABLE AND THAT FEELING IS AN EXCITING CHALLENGE. I LOVE HOW YOU CAN STOP IT, MOVE IT BACKWARD, GO UP, DOWN, SIDEWAYS.

flight time. For example, there would be a job in Nebraska. So, to get the helicopter from Pennsylvania to Nebraska, Bonnie would deliver it, and then the regular pilot would do the work. "I also flew some tour jobs with AgRotors, taking tourists on sight-seeing flights over the Civil War battlefields at Gettysburg." Pilots have to fly proficiency flights (three takeoffs and landings within 90 days) to carry passengers. Every two years they are checked in order to keep their license current.

After two years as ground support, Bonnie began to get a few spray jobs. "Flying spray jobs is high risk because you are flying at low level and high speed. You are dropping needed products and you must hit the target. It takes dedication to develop this skill. You have to be conscientious and deliver the material on target." Soon Bonnie was working half of the year on spray jobs. She was promoted to pilot.

Today, Bonnie spends about 60 percent of her time on spray jobs. She spends 30 percent on firefighting jobs—contracts which AgRotors gets and assigns pilots to work. At first, Bonnie flew on contracts with state agencies, which called for less experienced pilots. Once she got 500 hours total flying time and extensive firefighting time, she was eligible to work for the U.S. Forest Service. "I was one of the first women to ever work in this field and remain the only female helicopter ag-pilot. Now I have more than 7,500 hours of flight experience in a wide variety of assignments, although I have to admit, fires are one of my favorite assignments."

The rest of Bonnie's time is spent on miscellaneous jobs like charter flights, carrying external loads, or power line work. "The power line work is often a winter assignment, ranging from patrolling lines to detailed inspections, hovering adjacent to the tower and photographing the hardware, since ice storms and snow damage the structures."

The Wind and the Weather

On a typical spray job, Bonnie gets up, gets dressed, and is on her way to the job, which is usually "way out in the middle of nowhere," by about 3:30 a.m. Bonnie's company crew consists of her as pilot, a mechanic, driver of the tractor trailer that carries water, chemicals, and gear, and driver of the water truck. (The spraying can use more than 6,000 gallons a day.) A fifth team member drives the chemical company's delivery truck.

When the team arrives at the site, they prepare the aircraft, mix and load the chemicals, and are ready to begin spraying when the sun comes up. "Early morning is usually the best weather. The temperature is cool and the wind is light, so the spray will not drift to a nontarget area. To be so precise takes a skilled pilot and sophisticated navigation equipment. If the wind gets up to 5 miles per hour, we shut down operations. Often that means we spray until about 11 a.m., and during those hours we may have moved to four or five locations. Sometimes we have to shut down in less than 5 mph winds because of inversion conditions or high ambient temperatures. It is very restrictive."

When the crew stops spraying, the mechanic checks the aircraft and does any required maintenance or servicing. Safety is a primary concern of the crew members. After the equipment is secured, the crew takes a break. This can mean driving back to the motel they're staying in, visiting a local mall, or staying out and hiking in the area, and eating lunch—the only "almost" guaranteed meal.

Bonnie has learned to be prepared for down time and changes in weather. "I pack for cold and warm weather. I have two clothing bags, and keep one in the truck with me. I also pack my gadgets—books, a Scrabble game, hiking gear. When I have the tractor trailer, I take along my guitar and keyboard. I can't take as much when firefighting. There you have to take everything with you when you head out, because you don't know how long it will be before you get back to your base. I always take my high-performance kite. People think it's crazy until they try it. Then we all have a lot of fun until the wind dies down."

At 4 p.m. the crew is back at the site, preparing the aircraft to fly when the wind dies down, usually about 5 p.m. Depending upon the time of year, the crew will work until dark, which could be as late as 9 p.m.

Then they secure equipment and make the usually long trip back to the motel. Often the mechanic drives the fatigued crew.

"We do this every day without a break if the weather is good. If weather turns bad so we can't fly, that's an unscheduled day off to rest. If we've worked three weeks without weather breaks, we take four days off in a row to rest and recharge."

Fighting Fires

When Bonnie is part of a firefighting crew, her time spent flying must conform to regulations because she is working on a contract with the U.S. Forest Service alongside various state and local firefighters. "You can only work 14 hours a day; only fly for 8 hours; and you must have 10 hours off every day, and 2 days off every 14 days. Depending on the size of the fire, the number of people involved can range from a crew of four to numerous crews of hundreds of people. There are lots of pilots, so they can keep aircraft in the air all day."

On a typical day, Bonnie gets up at 6 a.m. She is a member of a HELITACK crew consisting of pilot and forest service crew. She works with these same people all year. The crew may be a single person or up to 20 or more. The first business of the day is a meeting with all the people involved in fighting the fire. They are 'briefed' about the status of the fire, the plans for the day, and assignments. Bonnie will be assigned which area to cover, given radio frequencies and ground contacts, and told about hazards and weather. She may be told to drop water on the fire or search for new fires.

"It's rewarding to see the results of the drop, see that you hit the target and made a difference." In her 60-foot, twin-engine Bell 212 (maximum weight 11,200 lbs.), she may carry as many as 12 people and deliver them via 250-foot rappel ropes to the ground to work the fire. She is in constant contact via radio, and when the firefighters are ready to be picked up, they build a 'helipad' in a clearing, and Bonnie lands and picks them up. When she isn't flying, she and the crew may do anything from mending fences to digging fire breaks, or they may read and rest.

"During the nine hours when we're on 'standby' (there is no fire we're assigned to), we have to be ready to take off in two minutes. It's like the city fire department. We may be sitting around playing Scrabble, my favorite game, but we're ready to be in the air on our way in two minutes."

Credit: Carolyn Russo

Mosquitoes in Manhattan

One of Bonnie's biggest spray jobs was spraying for mosquitoes in New York City in September 1999. Health officials discovered that disease-carrying mosquitoes were breeding in the area and could cause an epidemic of illness and death to the huge population. Bonnie was one of four helicopter pilots who sprayed 250,000 acres in the city and 135,000 acres on Long Island.

"We flew from dusk until 10 or 11 p.m., when the mosquitoes were most likely to be out. Because the city has so many bright lights, we could see quite well. But we had very sophisticated GPS (global positioning satellite) equipment on board and operated with a satellite guidance tracking system. It showed us exactly where we were and also provided a permanent record of the work. The New York Police rode with us. They flew the city all the time and were used to all the hazards, like tall buildings and other aircraft. We sprayed at the end of the runways at La Guardia and Kennedy airports, we sprayed city parks, and we finished the job in six nights of treatment."

The four pilots and their ground-support person received well-deserved recognition for accomplishing this difficult and important work. The Helicopter Association International awarded the group its prestigious humanitarian award for extraordinary service—the Igor I. Sikorsky Award for Humanitarian Service.

Bonnie has received many awards recognizing her accomplishments as the only woman in her specialized field of flying. She is included in the Smithsonian Air and Space Museum Exhibit, *Women and Flight*. "I hope this recognition makes the helicopter pilot job more visible so women can check it out and find out whether they might enjoy it."

Bonnie and her husband, Skip, own their own home near Gettysburg. Skip is also a pilot for AgRotors, where they met, and mostly flies to fight fires. In her spare time, Bonnie serves as secretary to the women's helicopter group, Whirly Girls. "I attend their annual meetings but don't get to spend as much time as I'd like socially, due to my busy work schedule. They have a great scholarship program for prospective pilots and established fliers. I received a scholarship in 1998 to take an instrument flying refresher course, which was an incredible opportunity."

GROUNDBREAKERS
The Pilot is a Woman

Harriet Quimby (1875-1912) was one of the first women reporters to write for a large newspaper (The San Francisco Call). On August 11, 1911, she became the first licensed female aviator in the United States. She died the next year at age 28 when her plane crashed.

The first African American woman pilot was Bessie Coleman (1892-1926). Trained in France, because no flight school in the United States would accept a woman of color, Coleman was licensed in 1921 by the prestigious Federation Aeronautique Internationale. In America she became known as Queen Bess, a celebrity performing in air shows and speaking out for the future of women in flight. She was planning to open a flying school for African Americans when she died in a plane crash.

Amelia Earhart (1898-1937) is the best known of the early woman pilots. She got her license in 1923 and became a national celebrity when she flew across the Atlantic in 1928, the first woman to do so. She flew many record-breaking flights, including the first solo transatlantic flight in 1932, which helped the public accept women pilots. In 1929, at the first all-women's Air Derby, a group of pilots resolved to work together to support women pilots. They named their international group the Ninety-Nines for the number of original members, and Earhart became the first president.

Sources: Ninety-Nines and Women's History Project

Ruth Marlin

Ruth Marlin

Air Traffic Controller, Federal Aviation Administration, Miami, FL.

Major in Labor Studies

Air Traffic Controller

The Voice in the Pilot's Ear

Ruth Marlin became an air traffic controller because of a combination of three things—timing, remembering the words of her mother, and reading an article in the *Smithsonian* magazine.

Growing up in Harford County, Maryland, Ruth enjoyed drama and was active in community theater. At school she liked science classes, so she thought she'd become a teacher. She entered college with that in mind, but during her third year she left school because she couldn't afford the expense. Ruth held many jobs the next few years and continued taking classes to earn her degree. But no job really excited or inspired her. Then, on a whim, she moved to Deerfield Beach, Florida, where her boyfriend had moved. She was driving to her job

Air Traffic Controller:
New hires entry-level
salary $30,500
Experienced controllers
salary range $40,300 to
$107,000

RUTH'S CAREER PATH

Likes science, theater

Works and takes college classes

Moves to Florida

selling advertising for the telephone directory Yellow Pages when she heard on the radio that the federal government was giving an exam for air traffic controller jobs.

"I remembered that eight years before in 1981, President Reagan had fired all the air traffic controllers. My mother had said I should apply for the air traffic controller's exam. 'There's a lot of security when you work for the government. Once you get hired, you can move around to other jobs,' she'd said. So I thought I'd check it out; I had nothing better to do that Saturday."

Takes test for air
▼ traffic controller

Passes academy,
▼ starts training

Certified, ATCS at
▼ Miami center

At that time (1989), there was a shortage of air traffic controllers, and the civil service test was open to all comers; you could walk in and take the test, no registration required. Ruth took the test and, knowing it would be a while before she heard the results, she took a new job in a chiropractor's office.

Within a month she received a letter saying that she had scored above 90 and was on the "fast track" and could anticipate being offered a controller position within 45 to 60 days. "When I received that letter with the applications and the security clearance information, the pages upon pages of paperwork were overwhelming. They wanted names and addresses of persons who still lived in all the neighborhoods where I had ever lived. I didn't know a lot of my neighbors and could barely get the information. I was frustrated and put the papers away.

"Later I read an article in the *Smithsonian* magazine (February, 1990) about the academy where air traffic controllers trained. The writer tried to make what people went through sound so horrible and grueling—having to learn so much in such a short period of time. But I thought 'That sounds so cool,' and I dug out the paperwork, finished it, and sent it in. If not for that article, I would not be a controller today."

Loves the Challenge

Despite the "fast track" process, it was about a year later that Ruth entered the academy. The first two months are pass/fail. It is a screening process. The program is designed to find out if you can learn quickly. "It was so challenging, so new to me, and so much to learn. I

quencies, air routes, navigational aids. They tell you that within a week you have to draw it from memory. Everybody freaks out thinking

YOU ARE PART OF A TEAM AND RESPONSIBLE TO HANDLE THE PLANES SO THE OTHER CONTROLLERS CAN ACCEPT THEM INTO THEIR AIR SPACE. HOW YOU SEPARATE THOSE PLANES IS UP TO YOU. NO ONE QUESTIONS YOU AS LONG AS IT WORKS.

enjoyed it. One of the first things you are faced with is the famous map test. They give you a map of the airways that shows tons of information—minimum altitudes, radio fre-

'there's no way I can do this.' But everybody passes, because the fact is you can do what you have to do. And the map test was one of the easiest things we had to do."

Ruth passed and went into a third month at the academy. Then she was assigned to Miami. "There is a risk you take, because they assign you where the jobs are. I loved it so much that I would have gone to Alaska, but I was lucky that there were positions in Miami so I didn't have to move."

Now the real training began—learning in the classroom, exposed to problems and solutions in the simulation laboratory, and actual on-the-job training alongside controllers. The training takes from three to five years, depending upon availability of the classes and progress of the student. Ruth was the first in her class, "a very competitive group," to receive her ATCS (air traffic control specialist) certification, called a pink card. Today, she is called a CPC, certified professional controller.

On the career path Ruth chose there are two options. You can choose Terminal or EnRoute. Terminal positions are either in the airport tower (what Ruth calls "swivel heads" who can watch the aircraft through the windows) or in the section called TRA-

CAREER CHECKLIST ✓

You'll like this job if you ...

- Are confident and assertive
- Are decisive and can make decisions quickly
- Are responsible
- Can learn quickly, like challenges
- Are good natured, have a sense of humor
- Like to be 'bossy'
- Can act confident even if you're not

CON, Terminal Radar Approach Control. Controllers here watch radar scopes to monitor arriving and departing aircraft and are in a dark room that may or may not be at the airport.

Ruth is in the EnRoute section and works in an air traffic center. There are 20 Air Route Traffic Control Centers in the country. The Miami center oversees 400,000 square miles of air space. It extends from Orlando to Havana, Cuba, and west to the middle of the Gulf of Mexico and across the Caribbean and Atlantic to the island of Grand Turk. "We control all space except that which is immediately around an airport."

Line 'em Up Like Ducks in a Row

Ruth works in a windowless room. The lights are low so she can easily see the radar display that shows her the 'blips' that are aircraft. She wears comfortable clothes and is dressed in a 'neat and professional manner,' usually jeans and a polo shirt. Her hours are regulated. She can't work more than 10 hours in a single shift; after 2 hours at a position she must take a break, and after six days she gets a day off. Since the center operates 24 hours a day, the controllers work rotating schedules. In Miami, they work two night shifts (3 p.m. to 11 p.m.), then a mid-day shift (10 a.m. to 6 p.m. or 11 a.m. to 7 p.m.), then two day shifts (6 or 7 a.m. to 2 or 3 p.m.). Every two weeks, they work a midnight shift (11 p.m. to 7 a.m.). "The midnight shift is always difficult, but you get used to it."

"I love what I do. The work is very satisfying, challenging, and creative. I get to handle things my way and use different techniques to solve traffic situations. When there are conflicts, when two or more aircraft want to be in the same place at the same time, I want to come up with solutions that benefit all the planes in my area.

"For example, say there are two aircraft heading toward each other. I am in direct radio contact with the aircraft and I talk with the pilots. I issue instructions so the aircraft won't come within five miles of each other laterally or so that they will be 1,000 feet vertically apart, above or below each other. They are moving at different speeds, maybe climbing, traveling at different altitudes. I have choices. I can get the airplanes to go around each other or one above the other. I have each plane's flight plan information on a piece of paper—a strip about one inch high and six inches long. It has the flight number, type aircraft, speed of aircraft, requested altitude, assigned altitude, destination, and route it will be taking. All this is in code on the strip—that's the first thing you learn, how to read a flight plan that's in code."

Ruth does have some limits to what she can do. "I have a designated piece of air space to work in. I am certified to work in seven different sectors. One of my sectors extends from Miami to Orlando and it's about 35 miles wide and ranges from 24,000 feet to 60,000 feet. I have sovereignty over that area. I can assign headings, stack the planes by altitude, and assign diverting routes. When all the planes are headed for the same destination, I determine

who goes first. You'll see a controller smile, sit back, then say 'Look at that. I just lined those babies up like ducks in a row.' We take a lot of pride in our work."

Strict Rules

The rules of separation between aircraft are strict. "If you have loss of separation, we call it an operational error. This is not necessarily a close call. If the aircraft are 4.9 miles apart instead of 5 miles apart, that's a loss. You are removed from your position, have to be retrained, and then recertified. If you have more than two in a two and one-half year period, you can be removed and fired."

The controllers have their own language. Some of it is slang. "One of my favorite sayings is 'cutting holes in the sky.' That's when you have to put planes in a holding pattern because they can't land right away at an airport for some reason. We don't do this often in my area, but some areas have to do it every day. It takes up so much air space for those big planes to turn in a circle traveling at least 250 miles per hour."

Controllers use a prescribed terminology when talking to aircraft. It is clear and concise and eliminates confusion as they give instructions. However, sometimes in an emergency or to advise about weather they may use plain language. Every controller in the world has to speak English for air traffic control.

Input into New Products

Controllers are members of a union—the National Air Traffic Controllers Association. Ruth is an active member and spends a lot of her off hours in union activities. She speaks to groups and attends meetings. She was chair of the legislative committee and wrote articles explaining new laws that might be passed. For almost two years she served as the union liaison to the Air Traffic Requirement Service (ARS), which meant she worked in Washington, DC, and had to be retrained when she returned to Miami.

Her mission at ARS was to analyze and help develop requirements for any new equipment to be used by controllers and to advise about what controllers needed in the field.

"This is a great program. We get controller input into new products early. Controllers don't have time to check in a book or hunt around for things. We need to be able to keep our specialization, same qualifications and pay grade. We're both active in the union, so whenever we can, we travel to union meetings and conventions. We also get involved in politics and campaigning and went to New Hampshire in 1999 for the primary."

Ruth enjoys spending time playing with Sean, who is five years old. "And I enjoy sitting on our balcony,

> YOU HAVE TO BE COMFORTABLE BOSSING PEOPLE AROUND. IT'S A FUN JOB TO TELL PEOPLE WHAT TO DO AND THEY HAVE TO LISTEN.

eyes on the display; so, well-designed, intuitive equipment is essential."

While working in Washington, Ruth traveled to Miami often to be with her husband, Scott, and stepson, Sean, at their place on the beach in Hollywood, Florida. "I met Scott at work. He and I have the same area of watching the ocean." Another activity that Ruth and Scott love is skydiving, but it is too expensive to do often. Ruth's work is a big part of her life. "When I'm on my way to work I think to myself it's just so cool. I don't just like doing the job, I like knowing that it is my job."

Karen Kahn

Karen Kahn

Captain, Continental Airlines, Houston, TX

Airline Pilot

This is Your Captain Speaking

As a girl, Karen Kahn loved airplane trips. She attended a boarding school in Arizona and often traveled by plane to school from her home in Carmel, California. Today she is a captain for Continental Airlines passenger flights, the pilot in charge of the plane. One of the first four women pilots hired by Continental in 1977, Karen flies throughout the United States and to Mexico.

Karen's flights leave from Houston, Texas, a Continental hub. She must commute from her home in Santa Barbara, California, to the Houston airport. "Pilots get travel privileges, but we don't get any real priority. The good news is that pilots can usually ride in the extra seat in the cockpit, unless somebody with more seniority than

Airline Captain:
Salary ranges from
$100,000 to $225,000
Flight Engineer,
Beginning Pilot:
Salary ranges from
$24,000 to $30,000
Aviation Instructor:
Earnings range from
$1,000 to $1,500 per
month

KAREN'S CAREER PATH

Gets private pilot's license, works at FBO

Gets instructor's license, teaches, flies glider planes

Forms pilot school with a partner

you gets there first. I have to plan to be at the airport early enough so that if I miss a flight I can take the next one." Karen and her husband, John, prefer to live in Santa Barbara where he is a captain for a regional airline. They met in Santa Barbara in 1982 and enjoy biking, walking, and flying together in their Beech Baron airplane.

Loves the Freedom of Flying

Karen loves to fly passenger planes. She likes the freedom, the travel, and the immediate feedback pilots get from doing the job right. She also likes that when she isn't flying, she usually doesn't have to think about the job. "There are training requirements, medical exams, and flight simulator tests, but other than that,

my free time is my own." She flies 80 hours a month. "If you also count the time waiting in airports, getting retrained and tested, and spending the night away from home, we put in about double that time." When she isn't flying, Karen often works for her own company, Aviation Career Counseling, writing articles or books or recording audiotapes with information about what it is like to be a pilot and how to prepare to get the job. She is the author of a book called *Flight Guide for Success*, full of advice on the best way to train for an airline pilot career. Karen also is an FAA (Federal Aviation Agency) Aviation Safety Counselor.

Because she has been with Continental for 23 years, Karen gets the route she wants more often than not. "I bid for the trips. They are awarded

Flies for Continental as
flight engineer, upgrades
to co-pilot, first officer

Co-pilot for
Micronesia Air

Marries John

by seniority. The schedule changes every month, so if you don't like your schedule one month, you can usually get a different one the next. When

as interesting flying over water on very long flights, and I don't particularly like hassling with customs and foreign accents. The nice thing about

SUCCESS IS AN UNUSUAL COMBINATION OF ASSERTIVENESS, CREATIVITY, FLEXIBILITY, AND PERSEVERANCE, ALL FUELED BY A DOLLOP OF COURAGE.

you're a junior pilot, you are on call 16 or 17 days a month and you fly when the airline needs you."

Karen's favorite route is from Houston to southern California and other West Coast cities. "I could fly a bigger plane overseas. I did it awhile. It's not

my airline is the opportunity for different types of flying for people with different tastes. Some people like freight flying, because they don't have to deal with people but love to fly. I chose domestic passenger flying because I like people and like being home a couple of days a week. I particularly like to fly to the West Coast."

She Makes Sure Things Go Smoothly

Karen's job requires excellent problem-solving skills. "As the captain you are responsible for everything. One day a private pilot friend of mine called me on my cell phone as we were on the ground before take-off. I said, 'I'll have to call you back. The flight attendants are having a fit because they don't have the extra attendant they were promised, they are missing half their meals, we've got a mechanical problem, and we still aren't fueled.'

"How do you solve all these problems and still get out on time? That's the challenge of it. Pilots are the coordinators responsible for making sure it all happens. I called up Operations that day to get someone over to do the fueling. I talked to the flight attendants about flying with one person short. We counted how many meals were missing and called food service. And we made sure the mechanical problem was solved before we took off. Handling multiple problems at once is something women are particularly good at. The biggest problems can come from miscommunication—when someone thinks the problem is one thing and it is really something else they should be paying attention to. Then you have to have good people skills and use your communications skills to explain the problem and how it's going to get solved."

Liked Math But ...

Karen left Reed College in Portland, Oregon, where she was a Political Science major, after two years because

CAREER CHECKLIST ✓

You'll like this
job if you ...

Are logical and organized

Can remember lots of things easily

Can take command and see that things go smoothly

Love to travel

Are fascinated with seeing things from the air

Will stay in good physical shape

Have good hand-eye coordination

Can work well under pressure

Will enjoy presenting a "corporate" image

she wasn't interested in school. "As a kid I liked math because it seemed very logical and orderly, but I made the mistake of not taking it my last year of high school. When I got to college and wanted to be a math major, I couldn't do it. I didn't have the background. Looking back, I wish I'd demonstrates your ability to learn difficult subjects, and they want people who will present an educated image to the public."

At 19, Karen was living in San Francisco after leaving college. A pilot friend told her if she wanted to learn to fly, go out to the local airport

IT'S A MISCONCEPTION TO THINK YOU NEED HUGE AMOUNTS OF MATH AND SCIENCE TO GET INTO THIS PROFESSION. YOU JUST HAVE TO LIKE THE PRECISION OF THE BUSI- NESS AND THE ORDERLY LIFE STYLE.

known about aviation colleges. That's a wonderful way to get your aviation training and your college degree. For me, not having a degree worked out because when I started flying the airlines were looking for women who just had the credentials; the degree wasn't as important. Today the airlines like pilots to have a degree. They feel it and give them five dollars for an introductory ride to see if she might like it. She liked her first lesson so much that she found a way to continue, even though her parents were less than enthusiastic about the idea of her flying. She worked in a secretarial job just to get enough money to fly. It took her eight months to get her private pilot's license. "This is longer than it would normally take, but I had to wait until I had enough money for each lesson. It's expensive. Then there is the cross-country flying. It takes you out flying for several hours and going to different airports, and that costs a lot more than just a one-hour lesson."

The year after she got her license, Karen landed a job with the local fixed base operator (FBO), the place that sells and rents planes, fuel, and supplies; conducts inspections; offers lessons; and generally caters to private pilots. "I worked as the scheduler and dispatcher and Girl Friday at Gnoss Field in Novato, California. I thought, here is a way to stay close to aviation. I knew I probably wouldn't get many rides in airplanes if I wasn't at the airport. Eventually I realized working for an FBO was a good idea because they let employees rent the airplanes at a discount. I wanted to get a commercial license so I could fly and get paid for it. I needed 250 hours of flying time. I also needed to get an instrument rating, which al-lows you to fly on cloudy days. Without it, you are really limited as to when you can fly.

"I was hoping that eventually I could get work ferrying airplanes across the country or doing mainte-nance test flights or patrolling pipelines. But the reality is that the people they hire for those jobs often have thousands of hours of flight time. Still I knew there were possibil-ities. I had a friend who worked for a pilot supply distributor and used to visit all the FBOs by airplane to take their orders for supplies or parts. I was hoping for that type of job."

Karen made friends with a local TV newscaster who came to the FBO to rent airplanes. He eventually pur-chased an older four-seater airplane, a Cessna 182, to do aerial photogra-phy for industrial films. Karen con-vinced him to hire her. "We did some interesting flying up to Canada and out to North Carolina to do filming. He would give me time off during the day to go to my instrument-flying lessons. It was good experience. I worked for him for about two years

and decided I was really interested in becoming a professional pilot."

If You Want To Learn, Teach

Karen got her flight instructor's license at the FBO in Novato, thinking it would help her be a better flyer and find a job. The FAA inspector who gave her the check ride suggested she look up an instructor at Sierra Academy in Oakland, California, when she expressed an interest in learning how to teach instrument flying. She took in-strument-flying lessons and glider lessons at the same time. "Because glider planes have no engines, you have to be more accurate, and that in turn makes you a much better pilot. Once I got my glider license, the place where I was taking the glider lessons, in the Napa Valley, asked me if I wanted to work there. I used to go up there on weekends and give rides. About that same time, I began doing instrument instructor training at Sierra Academy."

A month after she got her instru-ment-instructor rating, Sierra Academy hired her to give instruction. "I wasn't sure I could teach anybody the tricks of the trade, because I didn't know them myself, but my first student was a sort of know-it-all person who was getting his instructor's license. I made him show me things by demonstrating what he knew, while he thought he was learning from me." Karen taught a number of people how to fly, giving more than 800 hours of instruction and sharpening her own skills at the same time.

"The problem with being a flight instructor is that you don't get to fly a whole lot. You are mostly watching other people rather than manipulating the controls yourself. That means you don't get the flying time you need to qualify to be a professional pilot." So Karen got a job as a ground school instructor for a company in Tulsa, Oklahoma, where at least she could rent the airplane and fly to the places where the company was offering instruction. The company went bankrupt after she had worked for them for three months, but she and another man who worked there decided

to start their own school. They thought they could avoid the problems of their previous employer by offering quality classroom instruction to people interested in passing their written tests to become pilots. Accelerated Pilot Training was Karen's first aviation business.

The two partners bought a Bonanza airplane in Oklahoma City and began flying every weekend from Tulsa, where they were now living, to the West Coast, where most of the instructor work was. After about six months, they moved the business to Santa Barbara, California. "The huge preponderance of pilots live in the West." The business was so successful Karen and her partner were able to buy a newer airplane and employ two more instructors. They were giving lessons all up and down the West Coast.

After two years, Karen's business partner encouraged her to take the test to qualify for the Airline Transport Pilot's (ATP) license, because she now had enough flying time. She easily got her ATP certificate, "the Ph.D. of flying." She sold her interest in the business to her partner and started applying for pilot jobs with commercial airlines. The airlines had just started hiring again after a seven-year period in which they had laid off many pilots, and now they were hiring some women. When she applied at Continental, they were anxious to hire women pilots. It was 1977 and they had few women applicants who could qualify.

"My interview was a multiphase interview, including interviews with the head of employment and the captain's board. The captain's board (three pilots who fly regularly) grills you and plays good guy, bad guy. They wanted applicants to have a flight engineer license, because you started as the third pilot in a three-pilot plane, which is the flight engineer position. I hadn't taken the test yet, but I took it the next week and did fine.

"Then there were the psychological tests. They would give you a bunch of numbers in a sequence and you had to tell them which one was missing. It's easy when there are only a few numbers, but it gets complicated when they increase the numbers in the series. It was a test of how well you could remember things. There were other psychological tests, and then, when they decided you were a serious candidate, you had to come back and fly their business jet. I had never flown a jet, but mostly it was to see if you could be trained easily."

The Climb from Trainee to Captain

Karen was hired. After an extensive medical exam, she began training in a class of 16 pilots, the only woman. She was the fourth woman hired at Continental. The group went through two and one-half months of rigorous training, and Karen studied day and night. "I got some really good advice from a guy in my class. He said, if you don't understand it, memorize it, it will make sense later. And he was right."

She spent a year and one half as a flight engineer and then was promoted to first officer, or co-pilot. But shortly after that the airlines started laying pilots off again, and when that happens everybody gets bumped down a notch, so Karen was once again a flight engineer. Rather than do the flight engineer job and desiring to fly, Karen transferred to Continental's subsidiary called Air Micronesia, which flew in the western Pacific— Guam, Saipan, and Tokyo. "The flying conditions were very primitive. You landed on runways that were made out of coral. The terminals for passengers were thatched huts. The front half of the plane was freight and the back half was passengers. Because you were responsible for loading the airplane, you had to do all your own weight and balance planning, so you learned how things really work. But after six months I ended up back on the mainland flying as a domestic engineer again because they had laid off more people and someone else wanted that job."

In the early 1980s, Karen was laid off for three years when Continental declared bankruptcy and the pilots went on strike. She worked as a corporate pilot for an art collector, flying all over the United States, and to Europe

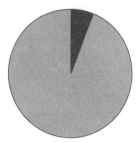

Of the 700,000 active pilots in the U.S., less than 6% (42,000) are women

Source: FAA and Women In Aviation, International

and Israel. One of the perks of this job was tours of museums, like the time in Jerusalem when the curator gave her and her boss a private tour of the Dead Sea Scrolls. "This was the height of corporate flying and a real education for me."

Karen got her old job at Continental back after the three-year layoff, preferring the commercial airlines to the corporate flying because it was more predictable and didn't depend on the whims of just the person who owned the plane. Two years later she was upgraded to captain on the MD 80, which meant being the boss and a big pay increase. She occasionally flies with a crew that is all female—a big change from being one of four in the entire company.

Getting Started On Your

Own Career Path

Getting Started On
Your Own Career Path

WHAT TO DO NOW

To help you prepare for a career in air and space, the women interviewed for this book recommend things you can do now, while still in school.

Aerospace Engineer, Joyce Rozewski

Take math, science, and computer courses, but also develop your communication skills. One way might be to take part in a play or a school program. Practice getting up in front of people talking about your ideas.

Read as much as possible about the space program and the people in it.

Air Traffic Controller, Ruth Marlin

Tour a facility. Sometimes the tower at an airport is too crowded so they do not offer tours, but every Air Traffic Controller Center does. Call the main administration telephone number to arrange a tour. Contact the union, National Air Traffic Controllers Association (NATCA), to arrange for a speaker who will talk about the controller career.

Check the FAA and union Web sites (www.faa.gov; www.natca.org) for information on current hiring practices. Right now the practice is to hire students that go to certain aviation schools that participate in CTI—the Collegiate Training Initiative that leads to an associate or bachelor's degree.

Airline Pilot, Karen Kahn

Visit your local airport and go for an introductory ride on a small plane. Start learning and becoming familiar with geography, map reading, and reading a compass. Begin paying attention to the weather you see on TV. When you are old enough, organizations like the Civil Air Patrol or the Ninety-Nines (women pilots) can get you doing hands-on things.

There are so many careers in aviation for women now. Mechanics is wide open because there are so few women mechanics and companies want them. Electronics technicians—avionics—is another wide-open field.

Astronaut, Kathryn P. (Kay) Hire

Be ready for any opportunities that might become available. Especially in space, there will be career fields that don't even exist right now. Make smart choices in the courses you take and the things that you do. Everything you do will have an effect on your later life. Don't do things that close doors for you, such as taking drugs. Choose things that will open doors for you in the future, such as taking advanced courses, getting good grades, and participating in extracurricular activities like sports or music.

There are so many wonderful web pages with information about space exploration on the Internet now. Look at the astronaut biographies to see what they studied in school and what types of fields they came from. Remember that in addition to astronaut careers there are all sorts of careers related to space—space chemistry, astrophysics, materials science, space medicine, and we even expect to be doing some manufacturing in space in the future. You'll find that most of us in space-related careers have multifaceted backgrounds, and that is especially true for astronauts.

Astronaut, Ellen Ochoa

One of the most important things you can do through middle and high school is to take advantage of the science and math classes offered. That is what will prepare you for a career related to space or engineering. Even if you aren't sure exactly what type of career you might be interested in, there are so many careers where it is helpful to have a technical background that you can never go wrong by having a good foundation in math and science. It doesn't lock you into working in a laboratory if you are not sure that's what you want to do, but it provides you with a lot of options.

If you are interested in aviation, you could explore flying lessons. There also is space camp, which addresses a lot of different aspects of this type of career—not only the technical aspects of how math and science might be applied, but also how to work together on a team to accomplish a mission and how different people with different backgrounds contribute to a mission. This emphasis on teamwork is a skill you won't always get in school, but which is very important.

Astrophysicist, Kathy Reeves

Science fair projects are great. There are lots of things you can do with astronomy and solar astronomy. Counting sun spots is easy to do. Take a pair of binoculars and have the sun go through the binoculars, but don't look at the sun. Just use the binoculars to project the sun onto a screen. They will magnify the image of the sun, and you can see the sun spots.

These are the cooler regions of the sun because of magnetic fields.

Cosmochemist/Planetary Scientist, Laurie Leshin

Get broadly educated in science. One of the things that I love the most about planetary sciences is that it is not just chemistry or physics or math or biology. You have to have a broad scientific background. Don't opt out of classes just because it might be the easier path. It's only going to get harder when you have to make them up.

Learn as much as you can and talk to people who are doing things you might like to do. If you love something, whether it's planetary science or something else, don't assume you can't make a career out of it. But make sure you love it. My field is very competitive.

Helicopter Pilot, Bonnie Wilkens

Check whether there is a helicopter at your local hospital or a sightseeing tour at your local airport. Perhaps there is a helicopter team at the local police department or Coast Guard or hospital. Visit someone who is involved with helicopters and ask what they like about it. Perhaps you can take a ride. When you are old enough, take an introductory flight, which may cost around $75. See if you like the 'feel' of helicopter flight. If you decide you want to learn to fly, don't be discouraged if it doesn't come quickly. It is hard to learn how to fly a helicopter.

Physicist, Mary Jayne Adriaans

It's important to be able to speak in front of a group. I didn't learn how to give oral presentations until graduate school, but I recommend learning these skills early.

Find out what you love to do and follow that. Don't give up on your dreams, and don't let anyone tell you that you can't follow your dreams.

Planetary and Astrobiology Research Scientist, Rachel Mastrapa

The best training before college is doing science fair projects. That is what scientists are doing every day. We are making observations, making a hypothesis based on those observations, and then doing an experiment to test the hypothesis.

If there is a university near where you live, contact the faculty about internships in the field that interests you. Sometimes our department will work with high school students to do interesting projects. I also get E-mail from students who just want to talk about my field.

Get good SAT scores in high school and get into a good undergraduate program. In the end it's the graduate program that is most important for the type of work I do.

RECOMMENDED READING

Magazines covering the air and space fields are varied and plentiful. Some specifically for women are *Woman Pilot* and *Aviation for Women*. Many of the books listed below are recommended by *Best Books for Young Adult Readers* edited by Stephen Calvert

Fiction

Alien Game by Catherine Dexter. (1995). Morrow $15.00. (New girl in 8th grade is from another planet)

Coast to Coast by Betsy Byars. (1992). Delacorte $15.95. (Adventure of 13 year old and her grandfather who fly a Piper Cub)

Frontiersville High by Stephen Bowkitt. (1991). Victor Gollancz $17.95. (Students visit orbiting high school lab in the year 2090)

Red Planet Run by Dana Stabenow. (1995). Berkeley/Ace $5.50. (Adventure of a feisty heroine and her twin)

Star Hatchling by Margaret Bechard. (1995). Viking $13.99. (A girl accidently lands on a planet and examines alien culture)

The Winds of Mars by H. M.Hoover. (1995). Dutton $14.99. (A 17-year-old thinks the president of Mars is her father, but he is an android)

Nonfiction and Biographies

Amelia Earhart by Doris L. Rich. (1989). Washington, DC: Smithsonian Institute Press.

At the Controls: Women in Aviation by Carole S. Briggs. (1991). Lerner $14.95.

Black Holes in Spacetime by Kitty Ferguson. (1991). Watts $12.40.

Coming Out Right: Story of Jacqueline Cochran, the First Woman Aviator to Break the Sound Barrier by Elizabeth Simpson Smith. (1991). Walker $14.85.

Maria Mitchell: The Soul of an Astronomer by Beatrice Gormley. (1995) Eerdman.

Pale Blue Dot: A Vision of the Human Future in Space by Carl Sagan. (1994).Random $35.00.

Queen Bess: Daredevil Aviator by Doris L. Rich. (1993). Washington, DC:Smithsonian Institute Press. (Bess Coleman biography)

Rising Above It: An Autobiography by Edna Gardner Whyte and Ann Cooper.(1991). Crown/Orion $20.00.

Secrets of the Night Sky, The Most Amazing Things in the Universe You Can See with the Naked Eye by Bob Berman. (1995). Murrow $23.00.

Pilots: The Romance of the Air: Pilots Speak about the Triumphs and Tragedies, Fears and Joys of Flying by William Neely. (1991). Simon & Schuster $19.95.

Space Travel by Philip Steele. (1991). MacMillan $10.95.

Stephen Hawkings Universe: The Cosmos Explained by David Filkin. (1997). Basic Books. (An explanation of the history of astronomy. It is a companion to the TV series.)

Vectors to Spare: The Life of an Air Traffic Controller by Milovan Brenlove. (1993). Iowa State University $24.95.

Women Aviators by Lisa Young. (1995). Facts on File.

General References

Encyclopedia of Career and Vocational Guidance. (2000). Chicago: J. G. Ferguson

Career Information Center (7th ed.). (1999). Macmillan.

Peterson's Scholarships, Grants, and Prizes. (1997). Princeton, NJ: Peterson's. Web site: www.petersons.com

The Girls' Guide to Life: How to Take Charge of the Issues that Affect You by Catherine Dee. (1997). Boston: Little, Brown & Co. (Celebrates achievements of girls and women, extensive resources.)

THE INTERNET

There are many Web sites that will give you up-to-date information about the U.S. space program and the many types of jobs that support it. Some sites have historical information about women and their achievements and some sites have biographical information about women currently on the job. You will also find information about books, videos, space camps for specific age groups, and educational programs available. We list a few of these sites below.

Aviation

www.ninety_nines.org (International Women Pilots)

www.wiai.org (Women in Aviation, International)

www.women-in-aviation.com (Resource center by author/historian Henry Holden)

iwasm.org (International Women's Air & Space Museum, Inc.)

Space and Science

Starchild.gsfc.nasa.gov (Service of the High Energy Astrophysics Science Archive Research Center within the Laboratory for High Energy Astrophysics, NASA, Goddard Space Flight Center)

spaceflight.nasa.gov (National Aeronautics and Space Administration)

jsc.nasa.gov (Johnson Space Center)

www.quest.arc.nasa.gov/women/bios/

www.stsci.edu/stsci/service/cswa/women (Space Telescope Science Institute, operates Hubble Space Telescope)

www.agnesscott.edu/lriddle/women (Agnes Scott College Biographies of Women Mathematicians)

www.physics.ucla.edu/~cwp (Contribution of 20th Century Women to Physics)

members.aol.com/Franknite/spaclink.htm (Aerospace engineer Frank Knight of Centerville, VA created this site to provide a noncomercialized set of links about space)

PROFESSIONAL ORGANIZATIONS

Many organizations and groups serve the aviation and science professions; many have informative Web sites. Here are a few to get you started.

AVIATION

Helicoptor Association International

1635 Prince St., Alexandria, VA 22314

(703) 683-4646 www.rotor.com

International Women Pilots, The Ninety-Nines Inc.

Offers scholarships, local chapters offer school programs, owns and operates the 99s Museum of Women Pilots at Will Rogers World Airport in Oklahoma City and Amelia Earhart's Birthplace Museum in Atchison, KS.

Box 965, 7100 Terminal Dr., Oklahoma City, OK 73159

(800) 994-1929 or (405) 685-7969

Web site: www.ninety_nines.org

National Aeronautic Association of the USA

Supervises sporting competitions

1815 N. Fort Myers Dr., Ste 700, Arlington, VA 22209-1805

(703) 527-0226

Web site: naa.ycg.org

Organization of Black Airline Pilots

8630 Fenton St., Ste 126, Silver Spring, MD 20910

(301) 538-0180; (800) 538 6227

Web site: www.obap.org

The Whirly Girls

Offers scholarships

P. O. Box 7446, Menlo Park, CA 94026

(415) 462-1441

E-mail: whirlygrls@aol.com

Women in Aviation International

Offers scholarships, educational programs

Morningstar Airport, 647 S.R. 503 S., West Alexandria, OH 45381

(937) 839-4647

Web site: www.wiai.org

SPACE AND SCIENCE

American Association for the Advancement of Science

1200 New York Ave., NW, Washington, DC 20005

(202) 326-6400

Web site: www.aaas.org

American Astronautical Society

6352 Rolling Mill Pl., Ste 102; Springfield, VA 22152-2354

(703) 866-0022

Web site: www.astronautical.org

American Astronomical Society

2000 Florida Ave., NW, Ste 400, Washington, DC 20009-1231

(202) 328-2010

Web site: www.aas.org

National Space Society

600 Pennsylvania Ave., SE, Ste 201, Washington, DC 20003

(202) 542-1900

Web site: nss.org

How COOL Are You?!

Cool girls like to DO things, not just sit around like couch potatoes. There are many things you can get involved in now to benefit your future. Some cool girls even know what careers they want (or think they want).

Not sure what you want to do? That's fine, too... the Cool Careers series can help you explore lots of careers with a number of great, easy to use tools! Learn where to go and to whom you should talk about different careers, as well as books to read and videos to see. Then, you're on the road to cool girl success!

Written especially for girls, this new series tells what it's like today for women in all types of jobs with special emphasis on nontraditional careers for women. The upbeat and informative pages provide answers to questions you want answered, such as:

✔ What jobs do women find meaningful?
✔ What do women succeed at today?
✔ How did they prepare for these jobs?
✔ How did they find their job?
✔ What are their lives like?
✔ How do I find out more about this type of work?

Each book profiles ten women who love their work. These women had dreams, but didn't always know what they wanted to be when they grew up. Zoologist Claudia Luke knew she wanted to work outdoors and that she was interested in animals, but she didn't even know what a zoologist was, much less what they did and how you got to be one. Elizabeth Gruben was going to be a lawyer until she discovered the world of Silicon Valley computers and started her own multimedia company. Mary Beth Quinn grew up in Stowe, Vermont, where she skied competitively and taught skiing. Now she runs a ski school at a Virginia ski resort. These three women's stories appear with others in a new series of career books for young readers.

The Cool Careers for Girls series encourages career exploration and broadens girls' career horizons. It shows girls what it takes to succeed, by providing easy-to-read information about careers that young girls may not have considered because they didn't know about them. They learn from women who are in today's workplace—women who know what it takes today to get the job.

EACH BOOK ALSO INCLUDES:

- personality checklist for each job
- lists of books to read and videos to see
- salary information
- supportive organizations to contact for scholarships, mentoring, or apprenticeship and intern programs

THE BOOKS ALSO LOOK AT:

- ✔ What skills are needed to succeed in each career
- ✔ The physical demands of the different jobs
- ✔ What the women earn
- ✔ How to judge whether you have the personality traits to succeed in the different jobs
- ✔ How much leisure time you'll have
- ✔ How women balance work and relationships
- ✔ Reasons for changing jobs
- ✔ The support received by women to pursue their goals
- ✔ How women handle pregnancy and child care
- ✔ What you need to study to get these jobs and others

So GET WITH IT!
Start your Cool Careers for Girls library today...

ORDER FORM

TITLE	PAPER	CLOTH	QUANTITY
Cool Careers for Girls in Computers	$12.95	$19.95	_____
Cool Careers for Girls in Sports	$12.95	$19.95	_____
Cool Careers for Girls with Animals	$12.95	$19.95	_____
Cool Careers for Girls in Health	$12.95	$19.95	_____
Cool Careers for Girls in Engineering	$12.95	$19.95	_____
Cool Careers for Girls with Food	$12.95	$19.95	_____
Cool Careers for Girls in Construction	$12.95	$19.95	_____
Cool Careers for Girls in Performing Arts	$12.95	$19.95	_____
Cool Careers for Girls in Air and Space	$12.95	$19.95	_____
Cool Careers for Girls in Law	$12.95	$19.95	_____
		SUBTOTAL	_____

VA Residents add 4½% sales tax   _____
Shipping/handling $5.00+ $5.00
$1.50 for each additional book order (__ x $1.50)   _____

                                          TOTAL ENCLOSED _____

SHIP TO: (street address only for UPS or RPS delivery)
Name: _____
Address: _____

❐ I enclose check/money order for $_____ made payable to Impact Publications
❐ Charge $ _____ to: ❐ Visa ❐ MasterCard ❐ AmEx ❐ Discover

Card #: _____ Expiration: _____
Signature: _____ Phone number: _____

Phone toll-free at 1-800/361-1055, or fax/mail/email your order to:
IMPACT PUBLICATIONS 9104 Manassas Drive, Suite N, Manassas Park, VA 20111-5211
Fax: 703/335-9486; email: orders@impactpublications.com